THE BAL

A proud, pow

Scandal has rocked the
Balfour family…

Its glittering, gorgeous daughters are in disgrace…

Banished from the Balfour mansion, they're sent to
the boldest, most magnificent men in the world to be
wedded, bedded…and tamed!

*And so begins a scandalous saga of dazzling
glamour and passionate surrender.*

**Each month, Harlequin Presents®
is delighted to bring you an exciting new
installment from THE BALFOUR BRIDES.
You won't want to miss out!**

Eight volumes to collect and treasure!

It was *him!*

Luc.

No, not Luc, Annie realized as she began to tremble, but *Luca de Salvatore.*

She had never even guessed, never imagined, that the Luca de Salvatore, spoken of with so much awe and respect by people equally as powerful as he—such as her father—was actually Luc! *Her* Luc!

No, not *her* Luc, Annie corrected shakily. He had never been her Luc. One night together four and a half years ago hadn't made him hers. And Luca de Salvatore, with a well-earned reputation for being coldly ruthless in his personal life as well as in business, had never belonged to any woman....

Carole Mortimer

ANNIE AND THE RED-HOT ITALIAN

The
Balfour
Brides

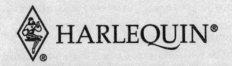

HARLEQUIN®

TORONTO • NEW YORK • LONDON
AMSTERDAM • PARIS • SYDNEY • HAMBURG
STOCKHOLM • ATHENS • TOKYO • MILAN • MADRID
PRAGUE • WARSAW • BUDAPEST • AUCKLAND

Special thanks and acknowledgment are given to
Carole Mortimer for her contribution to
The Balfour Brides series.

ISBN-13: 978-0-373-12964-5

ANNIE AND THE RED-HOT ITALIAN

First North American Publication 2011

All about the author...
Carole Mortimer

CAROLE MORTIMER is one of Harlequin's most popular and prolific authors. Since her first novel was published in 1979, this British writer has shown no signs of slowing her pace. In fact, she has published more than 135 novels!

Her strong, traditional romances, with their distinctive style, brilliantly developed characters and romantic plot twists, have earned her an enthusiastic audience worldwide.

Carole was born in an English village that she claims was so small that "if you blinked as you drove through it, you could miss seeing it completely!" She adds that her parents still live in the house where she first came into the world, and her two brothers live very close by.

Carole's early ambition to become a nurse came to an abrupt end after only one year of training, due to a weakness in her back, suffered as the aftermath of a fall. Instead she went on to work in the computer department of a well-known stationery company.

During her time there, Carole made her first attempt at writing a novel for Harlequin Books. "The manuscript was far too short and the plotline not up to standard, so I naturally received a rejection slip," she says. "Not taking rejection well, I went off in a sulk for two years before deciding to have another go." Her second manuscript was accepted, beginning a long and fruitful career. She says she has enjoyed every moment of it!

Carole lives "in a most beautiful part of Britain" with her husband and children.

"I really do enjoy my writing, and have every intention of continuing to do so for another twenty years!"

PROLOGUE

Italian ski resort, January 2006

'HAVE your friends all deserted you…?'

Annie, having been gazing apprehensively down the Italian mountain slope, trying to decide whether she felt up to the risk of skiing down her first black run, now felt a quiver down her spine that owed nothing to the danger of the slope or the chill in the air and everything to the sound of that huskily accented voice that spoke so teasingly behind her.

That quiver turned to a delicious shiver as she turned and took her first look at the man who had spoken. Very tall, and dressed all in black, with wide shoulders and narrow waist and hips, he looked like one of those male models her older sister Bella so often worked with. Except there was nothing in the least false or affected about this man's raw sexuality.

Black reflective sunglasses prevented Annie from seeing what colour his eyes were, but the rest of him certainly took her breath away. Shoulder-length dark hair showed beneath his woollen ski hat; the face behind the sunglasses was tanned, with high cheekbones and a long aristocratic nose above a sensually chiselled mouth, and his square jaw was strong and determined.

He gave her a devilish grin, his teeth very white and even against the dark swarthiness of his skin. 'Or perhaps you simply changed your mind about attempting this particular run?' he taunted.

That was exactly what Annie *had* done!

She hadn't been too sure if she wanted to come on this holiday when a dozen or so of her university friends had suggested they all go on a post-Christmas skiing trip to Italy before they settled down to studying for their final exams in the summer, but surprisingly the past week had been a lot of fun. The weather had been perfect. The skiing fantastic. And there had been a noisy party in their chalet every night, usually with lots of other guests staying at the resort invited to join them.

After years of suffering the fierce competitiveness of her sisters when they went on their annual winter holiday to Klosters, Annie had found herself blossoming in the more relaxed company of her friends. So much so, that today, with only three days of her holiday left to go, she had decided to attempt a black run. Unfortunately she had chickened out after the last of her friends had already set off to join the others for hot chocolate in the cafeteria at the bottom of the mountain.

Only to now find herself being challenged by this gorgeous Italian...

'I was just taking a breather,' she excused, not quite truthfully.

He flashed her a hard, knowing smile. 'Then perhaps you would care to join me in a race to the bottom?'

And perhaps she wouldn't! It would be foolish, totally reckless, to accept this gorgeous man's challenge. Wouldn't it…?

Foolish *and* reckless, Annie acknowledged. But after being practical and sensible all her life, wasn't it time she did something foolish and reckless, like following this sexily attractive man down a mountain? Of course it was!

Annie straightened determinedly. 'That's fine with me!' She dug her poles into the soft snow to push herself forward onto the run.

An experienced if only competent skier, Annie was no match for the skill of the man who overtook her within seconds of them setting off, his style much more daring than her own as he hot-dogged down the mountain ahead of her.

Needing all her concentration just to remain upright, Annie nevertheless found herself watching the sheer elegance of the man's style. He moved so smoothly, so capably, that just looking at him was exhilarating. By the time she skied to a halt beside him at the bottom of the mountain her cheeks were flushed and her eyes a bright periwinkle blue.

'That was fun!' She laughed up at him breathlessly.

'Yes, it was.' He gave her another of those devil-may-care smiles as he removed his sunglasses to reveal the deepest, darkest brown eyes Annie had ever looked into.

'Want to try it again?' she suggested enthusiastically, reluctant for this time with him to end. With three beautiful sisters older than her, Annie rarely found herself the object of any man's interest, let alone one as gorgeous as this one.

The man grinned down at her. 'I have finished skiing

for today and now it is my intention to return to my chalet and drink schnapps.'

The light went out of the young woman's deep blue eyes, her smile becoming noticeably disappointed. 'Oh.'

He looked down at her speculatively. 'Perhaps you would care to join me?' he asked.

'I would?' She blinked up at him owlishly. 'I mean… yes, I would.' She gave a firm nod.

'Luc.' He removed his ski glove before proffering his hand.

She returned the gesture, her hand small and warm in his much larger one. 'Annie.'

Luc had kept to himself since his arrival at the resort two days ago, but nevertheless he had seen the group of university students intent on having a good time. He had noticed this young woman in particular as she seemed to stand slightly apart from the antics of her friends. She was certainly worth noticing, with her long, rich chestnut-coloured hair, the vibrant blue of her eyes flashing whenever she laughed and the way her blue ski suit outlined the lush, feminine curves of her body. He'd been consumed by a curiosity to see the lushness of those curves without the ski suit.…

If nothing else, her joining him for schnapps might succeed in a temporary banishment of the mess Luc had left behind him in Rome.

'I will wait here for you if you wish to tell your friends where you are going.' He glanced across to where her friends were seated outside the cafeteria, chatting and laughing together as they enjoyed warming drinks.

'I— Yes.' Colour warmed her cheeks. 'How thoughtful of you.'

Not thoughtful at all, Luc acknowledged cynically, but merely an effort on his part to make sure that the night he was now contemplating enjoying with this young woman was not interrupted by her friends if they came looking for her.

He reached up and gently touched the creaminess of her cheek, instantly aware of the darkening of those wide blue eyes and the way her breath caught and held in her throat. 'Do not keep me waiting long, hmm?' he encouraged throatily.

Once again Annie felt that thrill of awareness down the length of her spine. Dear God, this man was lethal. Absolutely, one hundred per cent lethal. And for once in her so-far-practical life, Annie was going to be daring. Reckless.

And to hell with the consequences.

CHAPTER ONE

Lake Garda, Italy
June 2010

'I'LL be home in a couple of days, darling.' Annie spoke warmly into her mobile, totally unaware of the sunshine and beauty of the scenery of the lake outside the long windows of the bustling hotel as she hurried down the carpeted hallway to the conference room on the ground-floor level. 'I love you too, Oliver—oomph!' Annie was brought to an abrupt—and painful—halt as she crashed into an immovable object.

A warm, firmly muscled, very male object, Annie recognised as the free hand she had raised to steady herself came to rest on one broad shoulder and she felt the ripple of those powerful muscles beneath her fingers.

'I'm so sorry—' Annie's laughing apology strangled in her throat, her face paling, as she looked up into the coldly brooding, breathlessly handsome face.

No...

It couldn't be Luc!

Could it?

Annie felt absolutely stunned. Could this man really be the same one she'd met four and a half years ago?

Apart from the fact that she had only ever seen the tall and lithely muscled Luc in ski wear or casual denims and cashmere sweaters, and this man was dressed in an expensively tailored suit and white silk shirt with a silver-coloured tie meticulously knotted at his throat, he certainly looked a lot like the man Annie had met, and spent a hot and steamy night with, all those years ago.

Except…

That Luc had had shoulder-length dark hair, whereas this man's hair was cut short—in an effort to control the inclination it'd had to curl? But this man's eyes, dark as onyx in an arrogant and harshly uncompromising face, were the same. As was the long slash of a nose, and the chiselled mouth above a ruthlessly set jaw.

He looked identical, and yet, at the same time, so very different…

The Luc Annie had met on an Italian ski slope four and a half years ago had possessed a reckless glint in the ebony darkness of his eyes. His hard grin had betrayed that same air of devil-may-care that had drawn the quiet and—until then—eminently sensible twenty-year-old Annie to him, like a moth to a flame.

There was not even a hint of that dangerous recklessness now in those penetrating black eyes that returned Annie's gaze so coldly.

Eyes that also seemed to totally lack the same jolting recognition that she now felt…

Annie removed her hand as if burnt from the broadness of his shoulder as she took an involuntary step backwards. At the same time becoming aware that she hadn't so much as drawn in a breath since she had looked up and instantly recognised her fiercely passionate lover in this icily controlled man.

Annie took a much-needed breath. *'Scuse, signore—'*

'I speak English, *signorina*,' he bit out curtly.

Dear God, that voice...

No amount of steely coldness could ever disguise the voice that had once murmured husky encouragements against Annie's throat and breasts as she climaxed again and again beneath the fierce, possessive thrusts of his hard body....

It *was* Luc.

But a different, much colder Luc than Annie remembered.

Twenty-six-year-old Luc had been wild and restless. Everything he did—from skiing to lovemaking—had been possessed of a driving, single-minded energy that dared anything and anyone to deny him. The same single-minded energy with which he had set out—and succeeded—in seducing Annie...

No one looking at the man standing in front of her could ever doubt that he possessed that same determination of purpose. But now that energy was as fiercely controlled as it had once been wild, and his emotions were hidden behind a face that showed only an arrogance and ruthlessness that made Annie shiver as he continued to look down at her coldly from a vastly superior height.

Luc's patience, never at a premium, evaporated with each second that this young woman continued to stare up at him as if she had seen a ghost. Or her worst nightmare. Certainly not the reaction that Luc was accustomed to evoking in any woman!

A humourless smile curled his lips. 'Or perhaps it is *signora*?' he asked.

'No, you were right the first time,' she answered.

Luc felt a slight stirring of memory as the woman spoke softly. Her voice possessed a husky quality that somehow seemed familiar.

He took in her medium height and slender body, clothed in a black business suit and white silk blouse. Her hair was a deep chestnut brown secured at her nape, her face heart shaped. It was an arrestingly beautiful face with a small, uptilted nose, and sensually full lips above a pointed and determined chin. A face dominated by eyes as deep a blue as Lake Garda itself.

Again Luc felt that slight stirring of familiarity. 'Have we met before, *signorina*?' he asked slowly.

She blinked before giving a brittle, dismissive laugh. 'I don't know, have we?' she said, deflecting his question back at him.

Luc bit back his increasing impatience. 'I believe *I* asked first?' he pointed out coldly.

And he could go on asking, as far as Annie was concerned! All this time, all these years, Annie's worst fear had been that she would somehow, somewhere, meet Luc again. A meeting that she knew would complicate her life in ways she didn't even want to contemplate.

Now, by some terrible mischance, she *had* met him again, had met the man who had changed her own life forever—and he didn't even *remember* her!

The relief Annie should have felt was overlaid by a deep resentment. This man had literally skied his way into her life and introduced the normally reserved Annie Balfour to an intensity of passion and excitement she had never known before or since, before disappearing again just as abruptly.

Only for her to now realise that their time together, all those wonderful memories that she had never quite been able to put from her mind, had meant so little to him that he didn't even remember her.

Arrogant louse!

Her chin lifted in silent challenge. 'I'm sure *one* of us would have remembered if that were the case, *signore*.'

Luc wasn't so sure. The pallor of this woman's face, the angry resentment he sensed beneath her tone, seemed to tell a completely different story. One in which he had patently not appeared in a good light.

As the only son and heir of a rich and powerful Italian business entrepreneur, Luc's youth had been one of wealth and privilege, with his every wish being granted. As a consequence, Luc knew he had become arrogant, and possessed of an overconfidence in his own infallibility. A youthfully arrogant belief that had continued after he had proved to have his father's flare for business, and at only eighteen had been placed in a position of power within his father's business empire. Until the overconfident Luc had taken one risk too many and the whole of his father's empire had come tumbling down about their ears...

Luc's mouth tightened as he thought of that time. Of the past four and a half years when he had concentrated single-mindedly, often ruthlessly, on rebuilding that business empire until it was bigger and better than ever. Years when there had been very few women in his life, and even then only ones who had shared his bed for the night and been quickly forgotten afterwards.

Had the young woman who now stood before him in the crisp black business suit, with her chestnut-brown hair secured in that no-nonsense bun at her nape, the clear lines of her face bare of any make-up to enhance her natural beauty, been one of them?

Somehow Luc thought not. Unlike *this* woman, those women had invariably been tall and blonde, rich and vacuous socialites. Nevertheless, as he continued to look at her, that feeling of familiarity persisted....

His mouth quirked. 'You appear to have forgotten your telephone call,' he drawled.

Annie gave a startled glance down at the mobile she still held in her hand. The mobile from which a concerned voice could be heard squawking, if not the actual words being spoken.

Oliver.

In her utter shock at seeing Luc again, Annie had completely forgotten that she had been talking to Oliver when she had crashed into the tall Italian.

She swallowed hard. 'If you will excuse me?' She deliberately turned her back on the powerful effect of this man's close proximity, intending to escape to somewhere more private to continue her call.

Although she wasn't sure she was going to be able to talk to Oliver with any degree of normality after this chance, disturbing meeting. In fact, the sooner Annie was able to get away from Lake Garda—no, from Italy altogether—and the man she'd had a one-night stand with, who didn't even *remember* her, the better she was going to like it.

Deeply aware that Italy was the place where she had met Luc and behaved so impulsively, Annie hadn't wanted to attend this management course at the conference centre in a hotel on the shores of Lake Garda at all, and had only done so because her father had insisted.

A father who, still reeling from the death of Lillian,

his beloved third wife and Annie's stepmother, had become dictatorial with all of his daughters following the scandal that had rocked the family to its very core during the celebration of the centenary Balfour Charity Ball the previous month.

Annie froze as she felt strong fingers curl about her upper arm before she had chance to walk away. Luc's fingers. Long, elegant fingers that nevertheless possessed a compelling strength.

Fingers that had once caressed and touched Annie more intimately than any other man ever had. And which still had the power to send an electrifying jolt of awareness down the length of her arm and up into the fullness of her breasts. Breasts that, to Annie's embarrassment, instantly responded to the familiarity of that touch as they swelled inside her bra, the nipples pressing against the lacy material.

Annie's eyes, the deep Balfour blue eyes, were flashing a warning as she turned back to face Luc. 'Take your hand off me!' She spoke between gritted teeth, her face having once again paled.

Luc lowered hooded lids at the vehemence he heard in her tone. No, he had not imagined it earlier; there was definitely some resentment being displayed here towards him, a resentment he wished to know more of.

He made no effort to release her. 'Would you care to have dinner with me this evening?'

Her eyes widened as she stared up at him uncomprehendingly for several long seconds. 'What?' she finally snapped even as the colour rushed back into her cheeks.

Luc gave a brief humourless smile. 'I asked if you would have dinner with me this evening. In apology for having almost knocked you over just now,' he added, both of them fully aware that it was her lack of attention to where she was going that had caused the collision.

She gave him a speaking glance. 'Thank you for the invitation,' she answered drily. 'But no.'

Luc narrowed dark eyes, unaccustomed to being turned down by any woman. 'Why not?' he asked bluntly.

Eyes the colour of cornflowers, and surrounded by thick dark lashes, glared at him fiercely. 'Because I don't allow myself to be picked up by men I don't know in hotel hallways, that's why! Now would you please let go of my arm or do I have to call a member of the management and have them throw you off the premises for harassing one of their guests?'

That might prove interesting, considering that Luc's family owned the hotel!

'That will not be necessary,' he murmured even as he slowly uncurled his fingers and released her arm. 'The dinner invitation was no more than a gesture of apology on my part.' He shrugged dismissively.

Annie, having already been completely thrown by Luc's unexpected invitation to dinner, thankfully felt the easing of that tingling sensation in her arm and breasts once he had released her.

Just as she also felt slight disappointment that she couldn't—no, daren't—accept his dinner invitation...

Oh, no—she couldn't still be attracted to this man! Could she?

No, of course not! He had erupted into her life, taken what he wanted from her and then literally disappeared into the sunset.

As Annie had taken what she wanted from him?

With three older sisters, all of whom had made headlines in the daily newspapers at one time or another, and three younger sisters—four now!—who looked to be heading the same way, Annie was the one who had always preferred to remain firmly in the shadows of the publicity so often connected with the Balfour name.

A fact her father had been well aware of when he encouraged her to join her university friends on that skiing holiday in Italy more than four years ago.

To Annie's surprise, away from the pressure and publicity that so often accompanied being a Balfour, and the constant competitiveness so typical of a Balfour family holiday, she had found herself relaxing and enjoying herself.

Consequently, when Luc had flashed that dangerous grin at her and issued his challenge for her to accompany him down the steepest black run at the resort, Annie had been more than open to his heady brand of seduction.

So much so that she had behaved completely out of character after going back to Luc's luxurious chalet with him. As he had suggested, they had drunk schnapps together while cooking a meal, Annie wrapped in a glorious rosy glow as the two of them made love in front of the blazing log fire.

It had been a time out of time. When she could just be Annie. And Luc could just be Luc.

But who was he really? Annie wondered now as she glanced at him cautiously. Because, from the expensive cut of his hair, the tailored suit, silk shirt and tie and handmade leather shoes, he was obviously someone important.

Not to mention someone she had wanted to avoid seeing again at all costs!

'No apology is required,' she assured him crisply. 'Now, if you will excuse me, I really do have to finish my call.'

Luc regarded her with guarded intensity. 'I cannot help feeling that the two of us *have* met before,' he insisted.

'In another lifetime perhaps,' she retorted.

'Perhaps,' Luc echoed slowly.

There was something about the delicate curve of this woman's jaw, the deep blue of her eyes, the husky, sexy softness of her voice, that he *knew*.

Nor had Luc missed her response to merely the touch of his fingers on her arm. Her breasts had visibly swelled beneath the jacket of the black suit, the nipples pebble hard against the soft material of her blouse.

And he thought her eyes once again widened in alarm at his persistence in suggesting that they had met before.

'Will you be remaining at the hotel for long?' he asked curiously.

'The weekend only,' she replied curtly. 'But I'm here on business and expect to be kept very busy, so I doubt that we will have a chance to meet again,' she added firmly.

She so obviously *hoped* that they would not meet again, Luc acknowledged.

Interesting.

Having taken over as head of the family business empire four years ago following his father's near-fatal heart attack, Luc was accustomed to being hotly pursued by women intent on becoming his wife or, failing that, his mistress. Whereas this woman could not have shown her lack of interest in him any more clearly.

Which only increased Luc's own interest in her. An interest he intended pursuing, with or without her cooperation...

He gave a determined smile. 'I would not be too sure of that, if I were you.'

Once again she blinked, her creamy throat moving convulsively as she swallowed before speaking. 'Just talking to you has already made me late for a meeting.' She gave a pointed look at the slender gold watch on her wrist.

He shrugged broad shoulders. 'Then a few minutes more will not make any difference, hmm?'

The woman shook her head. 'I'm sorry, but I dislike tardiness, in myself as well as others.'

Luc knew she was not in the least sorry. In fact, she couldn't wait to get away!

The fiery snap in her stunning eyes, and the stubborn set of her chin, told Luc that she had no idea how her obvious determination to get away from him only increased his interest rather than diminished it.

'In that case, I will say goodbye. For now,' he added softly.

'We will not meet again, *signore*,' she insisted, the delicate colour that entered her cheeks now due to temper rather than embarrassment at her previous rudeness.

Luc found himself giving her one of his rare smiles. 'Fate has a way of deciding these things for us, I have found.'

Fate had already led Annie into behaving completely irrationally in this man's company once, and she had no intention of putting that temptation in her way ever again.

Yet, if anything, this Luc was even more devastatingly

attractive than the man Annie had met before. There was a hard ruthlessness about him now, a haughty remoteness, that challenged as much as it beguiled.

As for his smile...!

Those moulded, sculptured lips had pulled back briefly over white and perfectly straight teeth, in a familiar wolfish smile that, although fleeting, had nevertheless made Annie's heart pound harder and louder.

Despite everything, she realised with horror that she *was* still attracted to him!

Her mouth firmed. 'I really do have to finish this call.'

Luc's mocking humour faded as he recalled that she had been talking to someone called Oliver when they had collided a few minutes ago.

A man named Oliver, who, from the lack of rings on her long and slender fingers, had not yet made a public claim on this woman, despite the fact that she'd huskily assured him that she loved him too.

He nodded abruptly. 'I too am late for an appointment.'

The woman's smile was saccharin sweet. 'Then I really mustn't delay you any longer, must I?'

This woman needed to be put across someone's knee, and her bottom firmly spanked, Luc decided ruefully. Her bare bottom. Her lush and curvaceous bare bottom.

It was an erotic image that flowered and grew in Luc's mind and caused his thighs to throb and harden as he became fully aroused—something that hadn't happened to him in years at just the thought of making love to a specific woman.

Luc had spent years rebuilding his family's wealth and business empire. Four long years when he had allowed no other distractions, least of all an interest in a woman, to interfere with those plans.

Attractive as this woman was, Luc very much doubted that she would hold that interest for very long either. But her prickly nature indicated a passion that might prove fun while it lasted.

'*Signorina.*' He inclined his head in farewell, secure in the knowledge, in the pleasure, of her presence at Lake Garda for several more days at least.

Annie held her breath as she watched Luc's long and arrogantly confident strides until he turned left at the end of the hallway, leaning weakly back against the wall of the hallway once he had disappeared from view.

Dear God!

How had this happened? Why had it happened?

It had happened for the simple reason that her father, newly fired with a desire to guide the lives of his wayward daughters into less notorious and hopefully more worthwhile channels, had decided that Annie was to take a more active role in the Balfour business empire by attending this management course!

Her protest that she had no interest in taking on a more high-profile role in her father's management team hadn't seemed to matter a jot to him. As the only one of Oscar's eight daughters who actually worked for him, usually at the office complex at Balfour Manor, Oscar had just overridden all of Annie's objections by threatening to sack her.

Annie had known that he had meant that threat too. That Oscar was absolutely adamant in his decision that it was time—past time—that all of his daughters went out into the world to find themselves and what they really wanted out of life. Even if the majority of them, Annie included, went kicking and screaming!

Which brought Annie back full circle to her presence here at this glamorous hotel set on the shore of beautiful Lake Garda in Italy.

A hotel at which Luc, her ex-lover, was obviously also a guest…

CHAPTER TWO

'So, *signorina*, you have found time from your busy schedule to relax after all.'

Annie's heart jolted in her chest just at the sound of that sexily familiar voice, and she was grateful for the dark glasses that shielded the expression in her eyes as she looked up to see Luc standing beside her. She had been hoping for a little peace and quiet as she lay on a towel on the sand of the private beach in front of the hotel.

But she would obviously get no peace today. The man was gorgeous. Decadently. Wonderfully. Indecently. Lethally gorgeous.

Luc had been vitally and excitingly handsome when Annie had met him all those years ago, but the skimpy pair of black bathing trunks that were all he wore now showed an added toughness to the lean and muscled contours of his body.

His skin had always been the colour of mahogany. But his shoulders were wider, and more muscled. A light dusting of dark hair covered a chest and washboard abdomen. His hips and thighs were lean and powerful, and those black bathing trunks seemed to emphasise rather than disguise the telling bulge between those spectacular thighs.

Thighs that Annie had once been intimately familiar with...

She sat up abruptly, her manner instantly defensive as she glared up at him from behind her brown sunglasses. 'Are you following me?'

Luc felt only amusement at the accusation. Knowing that the flush of heat on her cheeks, and the way her nipples had hardened against the material of her blue bathing costume, was due to physical awareness rather than the angry indignation she wished to convey.

In truth, he'd had no idea she was even on the beach when he decided to indulge in a swim before his meeting later this afternoon. But as he had stood on the warmth of the sand looking for a place in which to place his towel, he had spotted that familiar chestnut-coloured hair that had seemed to glow a deeper auburn in the warmth of the midday sun.

Having swiftly established that it was the little firebrand of earlier this morning, Luc had been unable to resist the impulse to join her. To annoy her further perhaps? She did look so very beautiful when she was scowling at him.

The black business suit and white blouse she had been wearing this morning had not done her justice, Luc realised once he had crossed the beach to stand looking down at her from behind black sunglasses.

Her bare skin was tanned a pale gold, the top of the blue bathing costume cupping full and exquisite breasts, the thin strip of material that connected the top to the bottom of the costume at the front revealing the toned flatness of her waist and stomach above enticingly curvy hips and long, shapely legs.

'What if I *were* following you?' He answered her accusation teasingly.

A frown appeared between her eyes. 'Then I really would have to report your harassment to the hotel management.'

'Please feel free to do so,' Luc invited as he dropped down onto the sand beside her.

The fact that he seemed so unconcerned by the threat told Annie that he somehow knew she would be wasting her time in making such a complaint.

Just as her inner feeling of panic also told her that she was completely aware—achingly aware—of the hard promise of Luc's almost naked body so close to her own that their thighs were almost touching.

So close that she could feel the warmth emanating from his body. So close that she could smell his delicious masculine scent. So close she could have easily reached out and touched one of those hard and muscled thighs…

Her fingers clenched so tightly in an effort not to do exactly that, that her nails dug painfully into the palms of her hands. 'What is it you want, *signore*?' she asked instead. 'Surely there are enough willing women at this hotel that you don't need to harass the only one who isn't interested in you?' Annie hadn't missed the openly lascivious female glances in Luc's direction since he had joined her on the sand. 'Or is that the challenge?' she added in disgust.

An amused smile curved those sculptured lips. 'Are you not being a little unkind to these other women?' He ignored her second taunt.

'I prefer to think of it as being truthful,' Annie retorted waspishly.

He raised dark brows. 'And are you always truthful?'

'I like to think so, yes.'

'Hmm,' he mused softly. 'So, are you *truly* not interested in me?'

Annie felt her cheeks colour in a revealing blush. 'I'm not interested in any man who, when he's away on business, just wants a weekend fling while out of sight of his wife and family.'

'And if the man has no wife? Or family?' he pressed.

Her mouth compressed. 'Don't they all say that?'

'Do they?' he asked.

'Yes,' Annie replied. She may prefer to spend most of her time at Balfour Manor but that didn't mean that she didn't occasionally accompany her father when he went away on business. Or that her father's presence protected her from the advances of some of the business associates she met at those times. On the contrary; the often scandalous exploits of Annie's sisters seemed to have given most of those men the impression that all the Balfour sisters were open to seduction!

Luc gave her a hard look. 'In my case it happens to be the truth.' Children to inherit, and a wife to provide those children, would one day be necessary, Luc accepted. But he would choose his own time, and the correct woman, when it came to filling that position.

'I'm still not interested,' she announced.

He arched mocking brows. 'No?'

'No!' she said with finality. 'And I very much doubt you usually have to try this hard to seduce a woman into your bed either,' she added.

It was true that Luc usually only had to show the minimum of interest in a woman in order to make love with her. But of late, he recognised with a frown, those easy conquests had started to pall. To become boring.

To the point that boredom had succeeded in piquing his interest in this bristly brunette? A woman so unlike the tall and model-thin blondes he was usually attracted to? Perhaps.

He moved restlessly. 'You presume to know me that well?'

Annie gave a derisive snort. 'I know your type that well,' she claimed.

'Indeed?' There was a dangerous edge to Luc's voice now.

'Indeed,' Annie echoed tauntingly.

Luc continued to look at her for several long seconds, the colour burning in Annie's cheeks by the time he stretched his long legs out in front of him and leant back on his hands in the sand to turn dismissively and gaze out across the lake.

Giving Annie the opportunity to study him at close quarters unobserved. To once again note the changes in him. What had happened in the past four and a half years to change Luc from that young man, who had met every challenge with a recklessness that bordered on dangerous, to this remote and ruthlessly unyielding man whose every word and action proclaimed contempt for the very wildness he had once possessed in such abundance?

Why should she care what had happened to him, Annie instantly rebuked herself, when the same intervening years had taken their toll on her own life and emotions? When he didn't even remember their time together that had resulted in those changes in her life. When he didn't even remember *her*!

'If you'll excuse me, I think I'll go for a swim.' Annie didn't wait for Luc to reply as she rose abruptly to her feet and began to walk down the beach to the water's edge.

Luc slowly turned his head, his gaze admiring as he watched her fluidity of movement as she walked across the sand, arms lightly swinging, shoulders straight, her back long and supple, her hips gently swaying—

He sat forward suddenly, the darkness of his narrowed gaze arrested on her lower back. On the tattoo revealed just above the soft rise of her left buttock!

Luc's breath caught in his throat as he stared at that tattoo. As the memories of a lush body naked in bed beneath him, wrapped around him, riding him as the woman smiled down at him seductively and her breasts jutted forward temptingly, came crashing into his head.

He rose quickly to his feet to cross the sand in three long, determined strides, before reaching out to grasp her arm and swing her round to face him. *'Annie?'* he exclaimed as he pushed his sunglasses up into the darkness of his hair to look down searchingly into her face.

Once again the memory of those golden limbs entwined with his flashed graphically into his head. As did the silky softness of her skin as he'd kissed and tasted every inch of her body—the length of her back, that distinctive tattoo, the full curve of her bottom—before he had turned her over and explored the curve of her neck, the hard pebbles of her breasts, the gentle slope of her belly, the tiny nubbin nestled amongst the auburn curls between her legs as she writhed beneath him in the throes of ecstasy...

The sudden pallor of her cheeks, and the slight trembling of her body, told him all too clearly that this woman had those same memories—just as she had when they'd met earlier this morning!

His eyes narrowed furiously. 'You denied earlier that we had ever met before!'

Annie gave a bitter laugh. 'No, what I actually said was that surely *one* of us would have remembered it if we had,' she reminded him. And one of them *had* remembered; how could Annie ever forget? Yet obviously Luc had! 'Something obviously just triggered your own memory,' she added sarcastically. 'What was it?'

A nerve pulsed in his tightly clenched jaw. 'The tattoo,' he bit out.

Annie's eyes widened. 'My unicorn?'

Several of her university friends had decided to acquire tattoos during their first year at Cambridge, and Annie, with a desire to be accepted for herself rather than as a Balfour, had foolishly allowed herself to be dragged along too. Most of the other girls had opted for dolphins or butterflies, but Annie had known as soon as she saw the unicorn that it was the one she wanted.

How ironic that its existence should have succeeded in alerting Luc to her identity when nothing else had!

'Your unicorn,' he echoed grimly as he grasped both her arms. 'Why didn't you tell me earlier that we had met before?' He shook her slightly.

'And what was I supposed to say when you obviously had no memory of that meeting?' Annie hissed. '"Hey, remember me? I'm the woman you spent the night making love to when you were on a skiing holiday four and a half years ago before dumping me the following morning."?' She scowled at him. 'Somehow I don't think so, Luc.'

Well, when she put it like that…

Having spent the past few years deliberately blocking all memory of his ignominious fall from grace, and the dire consequences to his father because of that recklessness, Luc now clearly remembered the night he had spent making love with this woman.

Luc frowned. 'We need to talk—'

'I can't imagine why,' Annie interrupted derisively. 'So we were lovers.' She shrugged. 'I remembered it. You obviously didn't. End of story.' She grimaced. 'Now, would you please let go of me, Luc—you're causing a scene.' She looked about them pointedly to where several of the other hotel guests were now watching their exchange with open curiosity.

'Ignore them!' Luc rasped. He didn't give a damn what the other hotel guests thought of them. Or him. He only cared that for some reason Annie had chosen not to remind him of their prior relationship.

'I'm afraid I can't do that,' Annie snapped. She only hoped, once Luc had released her, that she didn't add to their curiosity by collapsing at his feet! Her legs certainly felt shaky enough for her to do that.

She couldn't believe this was happening. Why did Luc have to suddenly remember their brief time together? It would have been so much easier, for everyone, if she could have just attended the rest of the conference without seeing him again—without him remembering—before returning home to England with no one any the wiser.

That Luc had now remembered their meeting was a

complication she could well have done without. One that raised too many questions in her own mind...

The fact that he'd looked so grimly formidable at having remembered that meeting certainly wasn't reassuring.

Annie forced the tension from her body and permitted a relaxed smile to curve her lips. 'Let's not make a big deal out of this, Luc,' she dismissed lightly. 'It was a little unflattering that you didn't remember me initially, of course, but—'

'Stop it, Annie!' Luc said impatiently even as his fingers tightened on her arms.

'Stop what?' she asked, frustrated at his behaviour. 'It's great that you now seem to want to get together and discuss old times, but really, what would be the point when—'

'I said, stop it!' Luc repeated with controlled aggression. 'The Annie I met before—'

'The Annie *you* met, and who you've only just remembered,' she pointed out fiercely, 'was twenty years old and *extremely* naive!' She gave a huff of derisive laughter. 'I've grown up a lot in four and a half years, Luc. Enough to know when a man's only interest is in taking me to bed!' she added insultingly.

Luc felt the nerve pulsing in his tightly clenched cheek as he considered how she had learnt such a thing. Apart from that night she had spent with him, that is...

How *could* he not have remembered Annie when they met earlier this morning?

A part of him *had* remembered, came the instant answer to that question. An inner part of him had recognised both Annie and the huskiness of her voice. The part of him—that recklessly overindulged young man who had almost ruined his family and caused his father's heart attack—that Luc had long tried to bury in the deepest, darkest recesses of his mind.

Until he saw the unicorn tattoo on her lower back and all of those memories came rushing back with a vengeance.

Her hair had been longer four years ago, of course—a wild cascade of wavy chestnut curls that reached almost to her waist. Her body had been more youthfully rounded then too, her curves lush rather than athletically toned as they were now, and her face had also been fuller, the cheekbones not so defined.

But he should have remembered the deep blue of her eyes and those long dark lashes. Should have remembered how he had enjoyed the plump fullness of her lips when he'd kissed them. When she had kissed him, on the lips, and other more intimate parts of his body. He should have remembered—

'I was your first lover!' he exclaimed.

The colour flooded briefly back into those pale cheeks. 'Yes. Well.' She shifted uncomfortably. 'Everyone has to start somewhere, don't they?'

Except in Annie's case Luc had been both the start and the finish.

What would Luc say, what would he do, if she told him that a child had resulted from their night together? That waiting for Annie at her mother's home was a little boy of almost four, who had Luc's dark curly hair and sturdy body, and the Balfour blue eyes shining brightly in a face that also bore a very strong resemblance to this man?

To his father.

To Luc.

Annie repressed a shiver of apprehension as she looked up at him, having no doubts that the hard, implacable man Luc now so obviously was took no prisoners. It was there for everyone to see in the hard arrogance of his face and the cold, remorseless darkness of those black uncompromising eyes.

No prisoners perhaps, but if he were to learn of Oliver's existence, would Luc want to claim his son?

And if he did, what would Annie do about it? Oh, she wouldn't allow him to take Oliver from her, never that, but would Oliver want to know who his father was? One day maybe. And how would Oliver feel once he learnt that Annie could have told his father of his existence now but had chosen not to do so?

Annie needed time to think. To try to decide what to do for the best. For Oliver's sake…

'Would you please let go of me now, Luc?' she requested calmly. 'I think we've drawn enough attention to ourselves for one day, and I have another meeting to go to this afternoon,' she added.

Luc's eyes narrowed as his gaze raked over her face. A face that suddenly completely masked her inner emotions. 'In that case we will dine together in my hotel suite this evening so that we can continue this conversation.' He made it a statement rather than a question.

Her eyes widened. 'I really don't think—'

'Think what you like, Annie, but your agreement is the price for my releasing you now,' he added coolly.

'The price for—!' Annie glared. 'You really have turned into an arrogant snake since we last met, haven't you?' she seethed.

Luc gave a hard, humourless smile as he slowly

uncurled his fingers from her arm. 'Perhaps I always was one.'

'Perhaps,' Annie said, aware that the anger she felt was the only reason her knees hadn't buckled beneath her when Luc released her. This whole thing—meeting Luc again, torn between whether or not she should tell Luc about Oliver and what might happen once she had—was turning into her worst nightmare.

His mouth tightened. 'Humour me, Annie.'

'I have a feeling that far too many women have already done that!' she retorted.

He gave a rueful smile. 'Perhaps.'

Annie sighed her frustration with his obvious intractability. What should she do for the best? Should she tell Luc about Oliver or not? Not to tell him now that she had met him again seemed cruel to both Oliver and Luc, but at the same time Annie feared what Luc might do once he knew he had a three-year-old son.

She sighed again. 'OK, Luc, I'll have dinner with you this evening—on two conditions,' she added swiftly as she saw the triumphant glitter in the depths of those coal-black eyes. 'One, that I be allowed to leave when *I* want to.'

'And if you wish to leave as soon as you have arrived?'

'I won't.' She doubted she would be allowed to leave if she decided to tell him about Oliver!

'How can I be sure of that?'

'I don't lie, remember?' she pointed out.

'Very well, I agree to your first condition.'

She looked at him from under long lashes. 'Two, we dine in the hotel restaurant and not your hotel suite.'

He smiled mockingly. 'You are…nervous at the thought of being alone with me?'

Nervous didn't even begin to describe Annie's feelings of apprehension concerning spending more time with him. She was only agreeing to have dinner with him at all because she already knew this older and harder Luc well enough to realise this situation needed closure. One way or another.

Besides, if she should decide to tell Luc about Oliver during dinner this evening, then Annie knew that the whole of the Balfour family would rise up protectively at any attempt by Luc to take Oliver away from her.

'Not in the least,' she denied easily as she turned to pick up her towel and bag. 'I merely believe in the safety of numbers.'

'So you *are* nervous of being alone with me,' Luc drawled.

'No, I'm not.' She flicked back her shoulder-length hair as she turned to meet his gaze unflinchingly. 'I'm merely hoping that the fact there are other people around—as there are now—will prevent me from giving in to the temptation I have to slap that look of satisfaction off your arrogant face!'

Luc gave an appreciative grin at this fiery response. 'I will very much look forward to seeing you again at eight o'clock this evening, Annie.'

'Well, that makes one of us, I suppose!' she said smartly before turning to stride determinedly up the beach back to the hotel.

Luc remained standing where he was for several minutes after Annie had disappeared inside the hotel, his eyes narrowed in thoughtful contemplation. He had known her before. Intimately. So very intimately. And she had known him just as intimately.

The resentment and anger he had sensed in her this morning now made complete sense. The apprehension he had read in her expression a few minutes ago, almost a look of fear, did not.

What could she possibly have to fear from him?

Could it be that, like Luc, she grew hot at the memory of that night they had spent together? That she became aroused at the thought of the intimacies they had shared? That no matter how she denied it, they might share those intimacies again?

Or could Annie's wariness of him be for another reason entirely...?

CHAPTER THREE

'YOU'RE just in time,' the woman at the end of the row of seats at the back of the conference room commented as she scooted along so that Annie could sit down beside her.

Annie had been completely flustered by that encounter with Luc on the beach earlier—by her uncertainty as to whether or not she should tell him about Oliver during dinner this evening—that she'd had very little time to shower and dress in preparation for this afternoon's meeting.

Consequently she'd only just managed to get into the conference room before the doors were closed. She sat down hurriedly now as the head of the conference stood to make several announcements before it came time to introduce the guest speaker for the afternoon, her thoughts still on the dilemma of whether or not to tell Luc about their son.

Oliver was only three years old now, but when he was older he might come to resent the fact that he had grown up without knowing his father. He might actually come to hate Annie for not telling Luc about him—

'I don't know about you, but he's the only reason

I fought so hard to come on this course,' the blonde woman beside Annie said in an excited whisper.

Annie had no idea which 'he' the woman was referring to, although she somehow doubted it could be the sixty-year-old chairman of the conference, Daniel Russell. Not that she was particularly interested in the other woman's conversation. How could she be, when she was so churned up inside at the thought of what was best for Oliver?

'He almost never appears in public any more, you know,' the woman continued confidingly.

'Really?' Annie answered distractedly, her thoughts still firmly on Luc.

Obviously Luc was Italian, but he'd told her long ago at the ski resort that his home was in Rome, so what was he doing at a hotel in Lake Garda, of all places?

More to the point, how long did he intend staying here?

Long enough to have insisted Annie have dinner with him this evening, at least, so that the two of them could 'talk'!

'—a warm welcome to Luca de Salvatore!' Daniel Russell announced proudly.

Annie glanced without interest at the podium, her eyes then widening in disbelief as she stared at the dark-suited man who strode arrogantly onto the slightly raised platform to take his place so confidently behind that podium.

It was *him*!

Luc.

No, not Luc, Annie realised as she began to tremble, but *Luca de Salvatore*.

Oliver's father was Luca de Salvatore!

Anyone who was anyone in the world of business—even the usually stay-at-home Annie—had heard of Luca de Salvatore. It was impossible not to have heard of the man who had taken over the reins of his father's crumbling business empire several years ago, before ruthlessly cutting the number of employees of that business empire to the bone, and then proceeding to eliminate or simply take over any and all of the competitors who stood in the way of the de Salvatore business empire, retaking its place as one of the most powerful in the world.

Making Luca de Salvatore, as the head of that extensive and successful business empire, one of the most powerful men in the world...

Annie had never even guessed, never imagined, that the Luca de Salvatore, spoken of with so much awe and respect by people equally as powerful as he, such as her father, was actually Luc! *Her* Luc!

No, not *her* Luc, Annie corrected shakily. He had never been her Luc. One night together four and a half years ago hadn't made him hers. And Luca de Salvatore, with a well-earned reputation for being coldly ruthless in his personal life as well as in business, had never belonged to any woman.

She had to get out of here. Needed to think—

Annie froze on the spot, literally couldn't move a muscle, was held completely captive, as the piercing coal-black eyes that had swept so purposefully about the room now came to rest on her as she half rose in her seat, those dark eyes narrowing in challenge as he seemed to guess she was about to leave.

As if, somehow, Luc had known she was here...

The slightly amused curl of his top lip confirmed that impression. As the slow, mocking rise of one dark brow over those taunting black eyes now dared her to stand fully and complete her escape.

Damn!

Luc had been standing unseen to one side of the raised platform when he chanced to see Annie hurrying belatedly into the room to hastily take a seat on the end of the back row, once again dressed in a dark business suit, with a cream blouse, the vibrant chestnut colour of her hair muted as it was swept back and secured at her nape.

He had noted that Annie looked totally bored at the mere thought of spending the afternoon listening to yet another talk on business management.

It was too much to hope that maybe her lack of attention to the meeting was due to thoughts of the dinner they would share later this evening.

She had certainly looked less than pleased when Luc had stepped out onto the platform. In fact, her eyes had widened in alarm and her face had visibly paled, he noted grimly.

Eyes that sparkled with sudden anger, and cheeks that flushed with temper, as Luc's mocking gaze deliberately caught and held hers.

She abruptly resumed her seat to stare at him with a glassy attention that was fixated rather than genuinely interested in what he had to say.

In an effort to unnerve him as he had so obviously unnerved her when he stepped out onto the platform?

Possibly.

Except Luc was not a man as to be unnerved by the angry challenge in a pair of sparkling blue eyes.

* * *

'Our afternoon speaker has expressed a wish to be introduced to you, Anna,' Daniel Russell, the chairman of the conference and owner of the prestigious Russell Hotel Group, announced heartily from behind Annie as she attempted to move hurriedly through the crush of people in her haste to escape.

She had listened to Luc talk for more than an hour and then had to listen to him answer questions for a further hour. An agonisingly slow two hours when all Annie had wanted to do was get out of here and shut herself away in the privacy of her hotel suite so that she could get her jumbled thoughts into some sort of order. Away from Luc. Away from the mockery in those piercing black eyes that had returned to her again and again during the long afternoon.

Learning who he was had turned Annie's world upside down, and now he had the gall, the arrogance, to ask to be introduced to her!

Annie's eyes blazed with renewed temper as she turned to face both Luca de Salvatore and Daniel Russell, the latter a grey-haired man of her father's age who Annie knew slightly from his past business dealings with Oscar.

'It's good to see you again, Daniel.' She ignored Luc completely as she briskly shook the older man's hand.

'You too,' the older man returned warmly before stepping slightly aside. 'Anna, may I introduce Luca de Salvatore.' He beamed proudly. 'Luca, this is one of the team at Balfour Enterprises, Anna Balfour.'

Luc's face darkened ominously. *'Balfour?'* he echoed incredulously.

'One of Oscar's many daughters,' Daniel Russell explained pleasantly.

Daughters Annie knew that Luc had certainly heard of—or more likely read about in the more lurid of the tabloids!—if the way those piercing black eyes narrowed on her so grimly was anything to go by.

A polite mask swiftly replaced the grim one, Luc's expression now becoming totally unreadable as he offered her his hand. 'Miss Balfour.'

Luc couldn't believe Annie was Anna Balfour!

Or, more descriptively, one of the many daughters of Oscar Balfour who regularly made the headlines in newspapers and magazines for embarking on one scandalous escapade or another.

'Mr de Salvatore,' she returned with unmistakeable mockery as she allowed her hand to briefly touch his.

A nerve pulsed in Luc's tightly clenched jaw. 'There is no reason for us to keep you any longer, Daniel,' he gritted out through a clenched jaw as he continued to stare down at Annie—no, at Anna *Balfour.*

'Oh. No. Of course not.' The older man was slightly flustered by the abruptness of the dismissal. 'It really is good to see you again, Anna,' he recovered enough to add. 'I was so sorry to hear about Lillian,' he added regretfully.

Annie nodded. 'It was a tremendous shock to everyone.'

Daniel paused from turning away. 'I almost forgot to ask.' He glanced back at her. 'How's Oliver?'

If Luc hadn't been staring at Annie so intently he might have missed the slightly shocked look in her eyes, and the way her chin rose defensively. As it was he saw both those reactions, and wondered why she should react like that at the mention of the man she had been talking to on the telephone earlier today.

Perhaps because she would rather Luc didn't know about the current man in her life?

It was a little late for that when Luc had already overheard at least part of her telephone conversation with the other man where she had told Oliver that she loved him.

For the moment, one presumed; the Balfour sisters were not known for their fidelity or constancy. What they *were* known for was causing scandals and gossip on a daily basis!

Annie's maternally defensive response to Daniel's mention of Oliver had been wholly instinctive. Instinctive but stupid, she realised as Luca de Salvatore's hard black eyes studied her even more intently.

She forced a relaxed smile to her lips as she answered Daniel warmly. 'He's very well, thank you.'

The older man smiled back. 'What is he now—three, four?'

'Three,' Annie said tightly as she watched Daniel walk away rather than meet Luc's glittering gaze.

'Who is Oliver?'

Annie drew in a sharp breath before turning back to face Luc, forcing herself to meet that accusing gaze unflinchingly. She really would prefer not to tell Luc about Oliver in surroundings such as these!

Her chin slanted proudly. 'Oliver is my son.'

'Your—?' Luc's eyes narrowed icily. 'You did not tell me you are married!'

Annie moistened suddenly dry lips. 'That's because I'm not.'

'Have you ever been?'

'No. And so you are Luca de Salvatore?' she murmured, suddenly wanting to change the subject. This really wasn't the place to tell Luc that Oliver was his son too! And how dare he stand there and make judgements on her when *he* was the reason she was an unmarried mother!

'And *you* are Anna Balfour?' he came back coldly.

She nodded. 'Family and close friends call me Annie.'

Those chiselled lips curved into a hard, humourless smile.

'No doubt you refer to the sort of 'close friends' we once were?'

Annie felt the warm colour enter her cheeks. 'No doubt,' she bit out curtly.

Luc's mouth thinned. 'I find the Balfour part of your name of more…interest,' he grated.

Annie knew by the contemptuous curl of his top lip exactly what sort of interest he was referring to! 'As I recall, neither of us seemed particularly interested in introducing ourselves properly four and a half years ago, Mr de Salvatore,' she pointed out drily.

'What was that all about, I wonder?' Luc countered scathingly. 'A dare amongst the Balfour sisters, perhaps, as to which of you could lose your virginity first—I think not, Anna!' He easily caught her wrist in a tight grip as her hand swung up with the obvious intention of slapping his face. 'I think we should leave before you cause a scene.'

'Before *I* cause a scene?' she choked, tears—of anger or distress?—balanced precariously on long dark lashes as she glared up at him.

'Before either of us causes a scene,' Luc amended, his

fingers tightening about her wrist as he began to pull her along beside him towards the exit, knowing that his usual tight control over his emotions was in serious danger of snapping completely.

Anna Balfour.

This woman, the woman Luc had made love to over and over again that night four and a half years ago, was one of the infamous Balfour sisters. She also had a young son. A young son whom she admitted had been born out of wedlock.

Annie knew by the inflexibility of Luc's grip on her wrist, and the grimness of his expression as he easily pushed his way through the crowd of chattering people still gathered in the room, that she had little chance of escaping whatever came next.

Instead she trailed along in Luc's wake, managing to bestow a wan smile on the woman she had sat next to earlier as she raised envious brows at her departure. No doubt the silly woman thought Annie had succeeded in capturing the attention of the world-renowned Luca de Salvatore!

'Where are you taking me?' Annie demanded as Luc made no effort to come to a halt once they were outside the conference room, but instead continued to stride purposefully along the hallway to the lifts, punching in a code and then stepping into the lift when the doors immediately opened.

'We are going to my hotel suite. Do not attempt to fight me, Anna,' he warned as she immediately tried to extricate her wrist from his grasp as he pulled her into the lift with him. 'You will only succeed in bruising yourself,' he advised.

'Really?' she challenged. 'Are you sure about that?'

Luc's gaze remained steadily fixed on the flushed beauty of her face as he considered her challenge. Annie was about five feet six inches tall, but still six or seven inches shorter than he even in her two-inch-heel shoes, and her build, whilst lean and toned, was no match for his superior strength. 'Very sure,' he finally answered drily.

'Mistake!' Annie announced even as Luc felt the turning of her hand in his as she took a firm grip of his wrist and proceeded to turn him and twist his arm up behind him. Her knee was placed in the curve of his back as she attempted to push him down onto the lift floor.

At least, that was what she had obviously intended to do. Unfortunately for Annie, Luc had spent part of his rebellious youth wandering the back streets of Rome looking for mischief. An occupation which his father had warned would be the death of him if he didn't learn some self-defence. Luc had learned his lessons diligently and well.

Annie had absolutely no idea how it was *she* came to be the one lying on her back on the carpeted floor of the lift, both her hands firmly grasped in one of Luc's. She stared up at him dazedly as he pinned her there by straddling her hips with strong muscled thighs, and black eyes gleamed down at her with satisfaction.

Luc tutted mockingly. 'I do not remember you expressing a preference for rough foreplay four years ago, but perhaps your tastes have become more—'

'Earlier you didn't even remember *me* from four years ago!' Annie gasped accusingly, her efforts to shake him off only succeeding in pressing the hardness of his thighs into her more intimately.

More intimately? The man was already so aroused

she could see the fullness of that arousal bulging against the expensive material of his trousers!

And she could feel the heat of her own arousal in the flush of her cheeks and the shallowness of her breathing. The telltale tingling of her breasts. The warmth between her thighs.

'And now I do,' he murmured throatily, that black gaze fixed on the fullness of Annie's slightly parted lips, raising her captured hands above her head as he leant forward slightly, as if he were going to kiss her. As if he were going to thoroughly enjoy kissing her!

Annie eyes flashed deeply blue. 'Too late, I'm afraid,' she taunted, refusing to give in without a fight. 'We Balfour girls aren't known for giving a man a second chance.'

Luc's mouth tightened even as he quirked one dark mocking brow. 'No?'

'No,' she said defiantly.

'Perhaps we should put that to the test?' Luc mused huskily, his lips only centimetres away from hers now as those dark eyes held Annie's captive.

The warmth of his breath moved softly, seductively, over Annie's parted lips, an insidious, erotic invasion that robbed her completely of her own breath as she lay beneath the press of Luc's warm, highly aroused body. Then he moved slightly and his lips instead began to explore the sensitive column of her throat. A throat that arched instinctively into those searching, pleasure-giving lips—

No, she couldn't do this. She couldn't allow this! 'We're in a lift, for goodness' sake!' Even as Annie made the protest she was aware that her tone lacked conviction. That her breasts were aching inside her bra, the nipples already erect. That the warmth Luc must feel as he rubbed the hardness of his arousal against her must betray her heated response...

Luc lifted his head to look at her, eyes gleaming with laughter. 'Fear of discovery only heightens the pleasure, surely?' He deliberately removed the slide from her hair before releasing it loosely onto her shoulders.

'Not for me it doesn't!' Annie snapped.

Luc allowed the darkness of his gaze to move slowly from Annie's fevered eyes to her flushed cheeks and swollen lips. Before moving lower to where her breasts were full and firm against her blouse, the nipples clearly outlined. 'Yes, I can see that,' he taunted softly.

'You—' Annie's angry rebuke strangled in her throat as, still holding her captive, Luc lowered his head and drew one of her aroused nipples into the heat of his mouth, his lips closing about her and allowing no quarter.

Even through the material of her blouse and bra Luc felt that nipple swell and grow as he drew her in deeper. Then he began to stroke his hard length between her sensitive thighs, instantly feeling the way she responded to his rhythmical movements. Luc pressed himself against her harder, and then harder still, as Annie made little mewling noises in her throat in harmony to that erotic rhythm.

What was she doing? Annie wondered desperately as a sob caught in her throat. Damn it, she knew exactly what was about to happen if she didn't put a stop to this right now. On the floor of a lift, for goodness' sake.

An occurrence, if she and Luc were discovered, that would make all of her sisters' past exploits pale into insignificance!

Her fingers became entangled in the dark thickness of Luc's hair as she pulled him away from her breast—she would think about dealing with that telltale dampness on her blouse later. And the throbbing dampness between her thighs. 'Get off me, Luc!' She glared up at him furiously as he looked down at her with dark, hooded eyes.

Annie was furious with herself as much as with Luc. What had she been thinking? Except thought, she accepted with some disgust, had very little to do with what had just happened.

This man had been her lover four and a half years ago. A relationship that had resulted in a child. Her beloved son, Oliver.

'Get. Off. Me,' she repeated with renewed fierceness as her fingers tightened further in the silky thickness of his hair.

Luc ignored her hold on him as he looked down at her speculatively. 'You would prefer that we continue this somewhere more private?'

'Frankly, Luc, I would *prefer* it if I never have to set eyes on you ever again!'

Luc gave her a wicked smile as he glanced down to where he could still clearly see the rosy hardness of her nipple through the damp material of her blouse and bra. 'All evidence to the contrary,' he drawled mockingly.

Her cheeks flushed with temper. 'You arrogant bast—'

'Now, now, Anna,' Luc cut in as he rose easily to his feet and pulled her up beside him. 'Has no one ever told you it is unladylike to swear?' he murmured as he released her to calmly straighten the cuffs of his shirt beneath his jacket.

'I must have been absent from the nursery that day,' she grated.

Luc's mouth thinned. 'No doubt all your sisters were too!'

'You— Why hasn't this lift moved since we stepped into it?' she asked suddenly, starting to feel as if the walls of this spacious lift were closing in around her.

Luc shrugged. 'It is a private lift that goes to the penthouse suite of the hotel only. Only the occupant of that suite knows the code of entry.'

'And that would be you,' Annie guessed, her hair swinging forward about her cheeks as she bent to pick her slide up from the floor where Luc had dropped it.

He smiled wickedly again. 'As the owner of the hotel, that would indeed be me.'

The *owner* of the hotel? Annie should have realised as much after the way Luc had been so dismissive of her threats to report his harassment of her to the management. He *was* the damned management!

'So,' Luc drawled. 'Which one of Oscar's many wives is your mother?' His gaze swept over her contemptuously.

'There have only been three!' Her eyes sparkled at his deliberate insult. 'And my mother is Tilly. Oscar's second wife,' she added as Luc looked down at her blankly.

'Ah.' He nodded. 'She is the one that still lives at Balfour Manor with him, is she not?'

Annie drew in a sharp breath. 'She doesn't live *with* Oscar.'

She eyed Luc impatiently. 'If you must know, my mother was heartbroken after her second husband died, and so my father offered her the use of the gatehouse at the Balfour estate.'

'How civilised to remain…friends…with an ex-wife,' Luc commented.

Annie raised her chin in challenge. 'Yes, it is actually.'

Luc shook his head. 'And his third wife—Lillian?—did not object to this arrangement?'

Annie went very still. 'What *arrangement*?'

'Oh, come, Anna, we are all grown-ups here,' he jeered.

'You're implying…saying—' Annie broke off on a gasp, her face paling.

Luc looked scornful. 'It is no wonder that Oscar's daughters are so…so wildly out of control, when their own father sets such an example.'

He was implying her mother had continued to be Oscar's mistress during his marriage to Lillian, Annie realised numbly. How dare he? By what right did he judge her family? 'You know absolutely *nothing* about my father or my mother,' Annie seethed. 'If you did, then you would know that they are the best of friends. That my mother is the sweetest, kindest, wisest—'

'I believe you are protesting too much, Anna,' Luc mocked, far from over the shock of discovering exactly who this woman was.

Just the name *Balfour* was synonymous with scandal. With beauty, glamour and style also, Luc allowed grudgingly, but most especially with scandal.

Luc had spent the past few years completely avoiding the sort of publicity that the Balfour family, the Balfour daughters in particular, seemed to take such delight in creating. Hardly a day went by, it seemed, when one or the other of them did not appear at the centre of one scandal or other.

Admittedly, Luc never bothered to read anything that was written about them in the newspapers, deciding that they were a group of silly young women with more money than sense.

Much like he had been until four years ago?

Perhaps.

Although he seemed to recall there had been an even bigger than normal Balfour family scandal on the front page of every national and international newspaper the previous month. Something to do with one of the daughters being illegitimate…?

Oscar Balfour had so many daughters—seven, no, eight at the last count—that Luc was surprised that anyone cared about whether or not they were all legitimate!

His top lip curled contemptuously. 'Perhaps you would rather not have dinner with me this evening after all?'

Annie easily guessed the reason for the contempt she could clearly see in Luc's expression. Not only were her sisters always involved in one scandal after another, but Annie herself was the single mother of a three-year-old boy.

Whether to tell Luc that Oliver was also his son was something that Annie was still undecided about. Even more so after seeing the contempt Luc had for her whole family!

'You've decided we have nothing to talk about after all?' she said sarcastically.

His jaw hardened perceptibly. 'Nothing that would not result in more insults being traded between us, no.'

Annie felt the stinging heat of mortification in her cheeks. 'Never heard the saying about people in glass houses, Luc? I seem to remember that Luca de Salvatore was something of a wild child in his youth,' she added as Luc raised questioning brows.

A nerve started pulsing in his tightly clenched jaw. 'Fortunately, I grew up.'

'You aren't the only one who had to grow up fast, Luc—' Annie broke off abruptly, realising she had said too much when she saw the glitter of speculation in those narrowed dark eyes. 'If you wouldn't mind opening the lift doors now?' she prompted stiffly. 'I have some papers that I need to read through and fax to my father this evening.'

After Luc's reaction to learning exactly who she was, Annie also had a lot more thinking to do!

Annie had never confided the identity of Oliver's father to anyone. How could she, when until today she'd had no idea that the Luc of four and a half years ago was actually the billionaire businessman Luca de Salvatore! But she knew exactly who he was now. And that knowledge only made her decision concerning whether or not to tell him about Oliver all the harder to make.

Luca de Salvatore was a hard and remorseless man. A man who would maybe not want to just play the active role in Oliver's life that she was prepared to offer him, but to take Oliver away from her completely...

Luc gave a humourless smile. 'So you work for your father?'

'And I hate it,' she admitted immediately.

'Then why do it?'

'Why?' she echoed. 'Because, despite what you might think to the contrary, I needed a job to earn the money to keep both my son and myself. And working for my father was the job least disruptive to Oliver,' she added defensively. 'Besides, you work for your own father, don't you?' she pointed out accusingly.

Luc's eyes narrowed. 'My father retired some years ago and left the running of the company to me.'

Annie eyed him mockingly. 'Isn't it nice to know that nepotism is alive and well and living in Italy!'

Luc's mouth compressed at her deliberate insult. His father hadn't just retired; he had been forced to do so through ill health, leaving it to Luc to restore the de Salvatore business empire after he had almost ruined it. Almost? His arrogant overconfidence in business matters had been solely responsible for bringing that empire crashing down around their ears!

He looked coldly at Anna Balfour. 'In England too, it would seem.'

She sighed wearily. 'You're right, Luc, we're only insulting each other by continuing this conversation.'

That was indisputable. And yet...

A few minutes ago Luc had wanted this woman as deeply as her heated response had told him that she had wanted him. Damn it, if Annie—Anna Balfour—hadn't called a halt to that lovemaking Luc knew he had been perfectly capable of completing the act right here on the lift floor!

Such impetuosity, such stupidity, was completely out of character with the man he now was.

With the man he intended to continue to be.

CHAPTER FOUR

'YOUR son is three years and eight months old!'

Annie had opened the door to her hotel suite in answer to a sharp knock, staring up at Luca de Salvatore now as if transfixed. He was dressed casually this evening in faded denims and a black polo shirt, but the roiling fury emanating from that hard, muscled body and glittering black eyes gave him the look of an avenging predator.

She should have checked through the spy hole before opening the door! Shouldn't have just assumed that it was room service with the club sandwich she had ordered for her dinner! Should have—

What did it matter what she should have done before opening the door? The cold and furious Luca de Salvatore who looked down at Annie so contemptuously was more than capable of kicking that door down if she had refused to open it!

'Isn't he?' he bit out harshly as the flat of his hand knocked the door out of Annie grasp before he strode past her into the sitting room of her suite, the depth of his fury a tangible thing.

Annie winced, delaying facing Luc immediately by lingering to draw in several deep breaths before she quietly closed the door and turned around. One glance at Luc's ruthlessly etched features showed her those few seconds' respite hadn't changed the force of his blistering anger in the slightest.

Of course it hadn't. Luc wasn't stupid—far from it!—and no doubt he was perfectly capable of doing the appropriate maths and working out that Oliver was his son too.

The fact that Luc looked as if he were perfectly capable of strangling her with his bare hands and that he would enjoy doing it told her that he had done exactly that.

Annie ran the damp palms of her hands down her denim-clad thighs. 'I told you earlier that Oliver is my son—'

'While omitting to mention that he is also *my* son!' he snarled, a nerve pulsing rapidly in the pallor of his tightly clenched cheek, those black eyes blazing dangerously.

Annie moistened suddenly dry lips before swallowing hard. 'Isn't that rather a drastic assumption for you to have made considering…considering the tarnished reputation of the Balfour sisters?' she asked shakily.

Luc clenched his jaw tightly, his hands curled into fists at his sides as he resisted his inclination to take hold of this woman and shake her until her teeth rattled. To shake her until she cried out for mercy. To shake her until she admitted the truth to him.

He gathered his rapidly fragmenting control and took a deep breath. 'Not when I have seen the evidence with my own eyes, no,' he said.

'Evidence?' she echoed sharply, paling slightly. 'You can't possibly have seen Oliver since we parted earlier!'

'Of course not.' Luc's mouth twisted scathingly. 'I

had my assistant in Rome fax copies to me here of photographs of the boy from several newspaper archives.'

And been shocked to the very centre of his being as he had looked at those photographs. As he looked at images of a healthily sturdy little boy with thick and curling black hair, and laughing eyes the same magnetic blue of his mother's, in a face that bore a startling resemblance to Luc's own at the same age.

He was sure, certain, that this woman had borne a son from their brief time together four and a half years ago. *His* son!

A son whose existence she had chosen not to share with Luc!

'Why would you do such a thing?' she breathed.

Luc gave a humourless smile. 'Curiosity, mainly.' His mouth tightened. 'I had no idea that curiosity would reveal your perfidy! Would show that unless you also made love with my brother—a brother I do not have,' he added sarcastically, 'that your son also happens to my son!'

'I—'

'I seriously advise you not to even attempt to lie to me, Anna,' he said menacingly.

Her chin rose defiantly. 'I'm not one of your employees, Mr de Salvatore, and so thankfully don't have to take orders from you.'

'You will take more than orders from me if you do not cease this ridiculous charade and admit that the boy is mine!' Luc reached out and took a firm grasp of her shoulders.

'Take your hands off me, Luc!' she exclaimed.

'It disgusts me to even touch you!' He released her so suddenly that Annie thought she was going to fall over,

Luc's expression savage as his glittering gaze raked over her mercilessly.

Annie felt as if her legs would have buckled beneath her if she hadn't grasped the back of a chair to steady herself. 'What do you want from me, Luc?' she asked weakly as he stood far too close to her and towered over her ominously.

'The truth, of course!' he said.

'Why?' she asked warily.

He raised an eyebrow. 'So that I may begin the process of claiming my son, of course.'

Annie felt the heated colour drain from her cheeks and her mouth once again went dry. 'Claiming him?'

Luc's mouth thinned. 'He is a de Salvatore—'

'He's a *Balfour*!' Annie protested.

Luc gave a hard snort of derision. 'And the whole world knows what a prestigious name *that* is!'

'No less prestigious than your own past wild behaviour has made the de Salvatore name!' she snapped back, her chin raised in challenge.

Luc became very still. 'What do you know of my so-called past wild behaviour?'

Annie wasn't fooled for a moment by his apparent calm. 'I experienced it firsthand, for goodness' sake. I'm the woman you picked up on a ski slope, spent the night with and then dumped the following day and forgot about, *remember*?'

Luc continued to look at her through narrowed lids. 'It would appear that the only redeeming quality we have between us is our son—'

'Oliver is *my* son—'

'*And* mine.' Luc's voice became dangerously soft. 'A

fact that a simple blood test will no doubt prove if you continue to be difficult,' he added confidently.

No matter how much Anna Balfour might try to deny it, Luc was certain he couldn't mistake the evidence of his own eyes; he knew that the small boy in the half a dozen photographs he had looked at earlier was his son.

An heir who would one day carry on the de Salvatore name as head of the family business empire.

'He has a name,' Annie snapped.

Luc nodded. 'Oliver de Salvatore.'

She gasped. 'No!'

'Yes!' Luc insisted harshly.

Annie gave a protesting shake of her head, knowing that the full name on Oliver's birth certificate, Oliver Luc Balfour, was even more damning.

She moistened dry lips. 'I had already decided I was going to tell you about Oliver—'

'When?'

'Over dinner this evening.'

'Why do I find that so hard to believe?' Luc bit out scathingly.

Annie's eyes flashed deeply blue. 'Possibly because you choose not to believe it!'

This was worse, so much worse, than Annie could ever have imagined. Maybe if the Luc she had been involved with hadn't turned out to be the reputedly ruthless Luca de Salvatore, she might have stood a chance of fighting this. As it was...

She had absolutely no doubts that all of her family—her mother, father, as well as her sisters—would stand with her on any legal battle that might ensue over custody of Oliver; they may be a dysfunctional family at the best of times, but when push came to shove, the Balfour family stood by one another.

Except in this case Annie knew that Luca de Salvatore—she could no longer even think of him as the Luc she had met and briefly been bedazzled by—was more than justified in staking his claim as Oliver's father. There had only ever been one lover in Annie's life, so how could Oliver's father possibly have been anyone other than Luca de Salvatore?

She moistened dry lips. 'What do you want from me?'

'From you? Nothing! What I want is my son,' Luc growled.

'You want visiting rights? Joint custody? Just tell me what it is you want!' Her voice broke emotionally.

Luc drew back sharply as Annie's words unwittingly confirmed that Oliver Balfour was indeed his son.

He really did have a son. A beautiful dark-haired, blue-eyed little boy of almost four years of age.

Luc dropped down abruptly into one of the armchairs to stare unseeing down at the floral carpet as he took in the enormity of his discovery.

In all of his thirty years Luc had only ever given cursory thought to the day when he would hold his son in his arms. The first twenty-six years of his life had been spent in a whirl of decadence and overindulgence, and the last four Luc had been too busy rebuilding the de Salvatore business empire to think of anything beyond that. If he had thought of marriage and begetting heirs at all, then it had only ever been in the abstract, something to be contemplated in the distant future, once he was confident that the de Salvatore wealth and business prestige had been fully restored.

To learn that he already had a son, a son named Oliver that he had never even seen in the flesh, let alone held in his arms, was almost beyond belief. Almost.

Luc raised cold, narrowed black eyes to look at Anna Balfour as she stood in the middle of the sitting room staring down at him in wary apprehension. She was right to feel wary! Even now it was hard to believe this woman was the mother of his son. That her slender body had become ripe and swollen with his child. Her breasts would have become larger too, in preparation for that child's birth. Had she fed him herself from those engorged breasts? Or had the spoilt and capricious daughter of Oscar Balfour passed their child on to a nanny as soon as he was born? To be nurtured and hidden away in a nursery while she carried on with her own life?

Luc's mouth thinned ominously. 'What do you think I want, Anna?'

Annie swallowed hard as she easily heard the edge of menace in Luc's tone. As every part of her screamed in alarm at the danger she sensed in Luc's too-still body and the coldness in those remorseless black eyes.

But it was too late—far too late!—for her to even attempt to avoid this confrontation. Maybe if she had told Luc about Oliver earlier today rather than letting him find out in this way… It was no good thinking of what she should have done; she had to deal with here and now, not what-ifs. 'I'll do anything you want, Luc, agree to anything you want, if it means avoiding dragging Oliver through a public custody battle.'

He raised dark brows. 'What do you have that I could possibly want?'

She frowned her agitation. 'Stop playing games, Luc, and just name your price!'

He regarded her closely. 'You believe everyone has one, then?'

Her father certainly thought so—at least, as far as business was concerned. Had assured Annie on numerous occasions that it was only a question of finding that price. But this wasn't a business deal. She and Luc were talking about their son's future, not some inanimate object. And Luca de Salvatore was rich enough, powerful enough, to make a good case for taking custody of Oliver if that was the route he decided to take. A route that Annie wished to avoid if at all possible.

'I've usually found that to be the case, yes,' she answered cautiously.

'And you are willing to give me anything, Anna?'

The hairs on the nape of Annie's neck rose in alarm at the danger she once again sensed in the very softness of Luc's tone. But what choice did she have? What choice was Luc giving her!

'Anything,' she echoed huskily.

Luc stared at her unblinkingly. Relentlessly. 'You love Oliver that much?'

'Well, of course I love him that much!' she answered impatiently. 'What sort of mother do you think I am?'

'I have no idea what sort of mother you are,' he cut in harshly. 'At the moment you appear to be an absent one.'

'Oliver is at home, with my mother—'

'That would be Oscar Balfour's second wife who has lived conveniently close to him in the gatehouse at Balfour Manor since the death of her second husband?' Luc drawled insultingly.

'*I* live in the gatehouse at Balfour Manor too!' Annie said resentfully. 'As does Oliver.'

'Could the reason for that be because Oscar Balfour prefers to keep his only grandchild, a grandson born out of wedlock, hidden away from the public eye?' Luc's voice was steely at the thought of his son being treated in such a way.

There had been very little information for Luc's assistant to find and send to him on Oliver Balfour. Just the name of his mother and when he was born, and those few photographs that the press occasionally managed to snap of him when he appeared at one family occasion or another. Other than those things there was very little known about the young boy. Certainly any mention of who his father was had been conspicuous in its absence!

The hastily compiled file he had demanded Marco gather for him on Anna Balfour was even less informative.

'Of course my father hasn't hidden Oliver away.' She snorted in disgust. 'As you say, Oliver is my father's only grandchild, and he absolutely adores him,' she said.

Luc nodded tersely. 'So much so, it would seem, that Oliver very rarely leaves Balfour Manor.'

'I'm the one responsible for that decision,' she said agitatedly.

'Why?'

She made an impatient movement. 'Because— Well, because—'

'Yes?'

How could Annie explain to this man—this hard, intractable man!—what it was like to be a Balfour? How almost from the cradle, it seemed, her every word and movement had been avidly followed by the paparazzi, to become front-page headlines in one tabloid or another? How much she had always hated it all? How she had decided from the beginning that she didn't want any of that for Oliver?

She sat down heavily. 'He's a little boy, Luc. A little boy who deserves to enjoy being a child rather than living the nightmare of publicity that has always dogged my own life.'

'There are ways to avoid such publicity—'

'Then I wish you would tell me what those ways are,' Annie snapped.

'Perhaps having less notorious sisters may have helped?' Luc pointed out.

Colour warmed her cheeks. 'I'm not responsible for the behaviour of my sisters!'

'No, you are only responsible for your own actions,' he allowed. 'So tell me, Anna Balfour, what do you think would recompense me for not even knowing of my son's existence for the first three years and eight months of his life?'

When he put it like that…

There was no way Annie could make up to Luc for missing those first years and months of Oliver's life. Nothing Annie could say, or do, that could ever bring that time back. It was already gone.

'I had no idea who you were, so how was I supposed to tell you I was pregnant, let alone inform you of Oliver's birth?' Annie reasoned.

Luc couldn't deny the truth of that particular argument, knew that when they'd met before they had both been living only for the moment. Luc because he desperately wanted not to even think of the mess he had left behind him in Rome. Anna Balfour because— He had no idea what she had been running away from four and a half years ago.…

Although perhaps her remark about 'the nightmare of publicity that has always dogged my own life' went some way to answering that question.

None of which altered the fact that Oliver was almost four years old and had yet to even meet his father!

Luc's mouth thinned. 'Did you even *try* to find out who I was? Once you learned of your pregnancy, did you go back to the ski resort and make the necessary enquiries to see if you could learn the identity of your lover?'

Her gaze no longer met his. 'No.'

'Why not? You can't tell me that with all the Balfour resources available to you, you couldn't have done it,' Luc pressed.

Annie stood restlessly, her eyes blazing deeply blue as she glared down at him. 'What would have been the point? We had a one-night stand, Luc,' she expanded. 'I can't think of any man who would have been interested in learning that a child had resulted from such a brief relationship.'

He scowled darkly. 'You are looking at him. As I am now looking at Anna Balfour. Really looking,' he added coldly. 'And I do not very much like what I see.'

Annie felt a sinking, sick sensation in her stomach. 'Stop calling me Anna Balfour in that insulting tone!'

Luc shrugged broad shoulders. 'I have only just learnt it is your name.'

'We both know that isn't the reason you keep saying it in that distasteful way.'

'Do we?'

'Yes!' Annie stared down at him in utter frustration. 'I'm sorry, OK?'

His mouth twisted derisively. 'Sorry that we chanced to meet again and I discovered the truth perhaps?'

'Yes. No!' She gave an agitated shake of her head. 'Maybe you're right, and I should have tried to find out who you were four years ago. I just—I'm sorry you never knew of Oliver's existence until today. I'm just sorry,' she added shakily.

Luc looked at her through narrowed lids, noting the shadows in those deep blue eyes, and the tears that glistened on the length of her dark lashes. Her face was deathly pale, and there was a slight tremble to those full and sensuous lips.

Yes, she was indeed sorry for denying him knowledge of his son these past four years. She was going to be sorrier still…

'Very well.' Luc stood. 'You are booked on a flight back to London on Monday morning—'

'How did you know that?' she gasped.

'Because before coming here I made it my business to know.'

Annie swallowed hard. 'Why did you do that?'

'The why is unimportant,' Luc said dismissively. 'You will cancel your seat on that flight—'

'No, I—'

'You will find that you and I will deal better together if you cease arguing with me over every little detail,' he reproved.

'My going back to England on Monday isn't a "little detail",' Annie insisted stubbornly. She needed to go home. Needed to be with Oliver. To take his sturdy little body in her arms and just hold on to him!

'I do not remember saying you would not be returning to England. Did I say that?'

Annie frowned her confusion. 'Well… no. But—'

'We will *both* be flying to England tomorrow, Anna,' Luc informed her arrogantly.

She moistened her lips nervously. 'Tomorrow?'

He nodded curtly. 'I will make arrangements for the de Salvatore jet to transport us there in the morning. After which we will both go to Balfour Manor and you will introduce me to my son.' His voice had hardened angrily.

Annie's mouth opened but no words came out. Luc couldn't be serious about coming to Balfour Manor with her! Couldn't expect her to just take him there and— 'Introduce you to him as what?' she asked warily.

He was every inch the arrogant Luca de Salvatore as he looked down the length of his aristocratic nose at her. 'As his father, of course.'

'I can't do that, Luc,' she protested. 'Can't you see that would only confuse him?' she reasoned as Luc remained completely unmoved by that impassioned protest. 'At the moment Oliver has no real concept of what it means to even have a father—'

'And whose fault is that?' Luc asked.

'Mine,' Annie allowed with a weary sigh. 'But if you come back to England with me tomorrow, and I introduce you to Oliver as his father, then he's just going to be confused when you have to leave him to return home a few days later.'

Luc looked at her coldly. 'I do not remember saying that I intended to leave him again.'

'But of course you will!' Annie exclaimed. 'You live in Rome, and Oliver lives with me in England—'

'Hmm.'

Annie tensed. 'Hmm, what?'

'Hmm, I have reached a decision on my "price" for allowing you to keep Oliver with you,' Luc informed her coolly.

One look at the hardness of those merciless black eyes and the cruel twist to those sculptured lips and Annie knew she wasn't going to like Luc's 'price' at all!

She swallowed hard. 'Which is?'

'The solution is obvious once you look at the situation logically.'

'Logically?' she echoed slowly.

Luc gave an arrogant inclination of his head. 'The only way that Oliver can both remain with you *and* know his father is if the two of us marry.'

'If—? If the two of us—? If we—?' Annie sat down again before she fell down!

Surely Luca de Salvatore, a man usually so assured and coldly controlled, had gone slightly insane?

Slightly?

Luc had gone *seriously* insane if he thought for one moment that Annie would ever agree to marry him!

CHAPTER FIVE

'No!'

Luc raised dark brows. 'No?'

'No,' she repeated firmly.

Luc calmly returned the fierceness of her gaze. 'No, the answer is not logical? Or no, you will not marry me?'

'Both!' she answered vehemently.

Luc considered her with complete detachment. Anna Balfour was without doubt a very beautiful and self-assured young woman. She also now possessed the sort of slender elegance that ensured she would look good in anything. She even managed to look sexily attractive in faded jeans that fitted low on her hips, and a fitted white T-shirt that barely covered the flatness of her stomach!

Yes, she was very beautiful. She also possessed an innate self-confidence that would ensure she felt comfortable in any company she happened to find herself in. The file Luc's assistant had hastily compiled on her also revealed that, despite being six months pregnant at the time, she had completed and attained a degree in English, attesting to her determination as well as her intelligence.

Despite all those positive attributes—and the physical

attraction that had drawn him to her this morning—Anna Balfour was not the woman Luc would have chosen as his wife.

Any more, it seemed, than Luc was the man she would have chosen as her husband!

His mouth firmed. 'A few minutes ago you promised to give me anything, Anna,' he reminded her.

'If you would let me continue to bring Oliver up in England,' she pointed out.

He looked at her scathingly. 'We both know that is not going to happen.'

'I—' Annie broke off impatiently, having no doubts now; Luc really had gone insane! 'Marriage is a little drastic, don't you think?' She raised incredulous eyebrows.

'You have another, less drastic, solution to this problem perhaps?' he prompted coolly.

It was that very coldness that unnerved Annie the most. If Luc's anger had been hot and accusing she could maybe have tried reasoning with him. As it was, his very calmness, that stillness of the predator he had so reminded her of earlier, told her that he was perfectly serious about his preposterous proposal.

She sighed. 'I'm only twenty-four years old, Luc, and I have no intention of marrying any man for the sake of convenience.'

'I do not find the idea of a marriage between the two of us in the least convenient either,' he admitted.

'Then—'

'Are you willing to give up our son to me?' he asked.

Annie gasped. 'No, of course not!'

Luc gave an unconcerned shrug. 'Then the matter

is settled. Once in England I will see to the necessary arrangements for our marriage—'

'The matter is most certainly not *settled*,' Annie interrupted as she once again stood. 'I'm not marrying you, Luc,' she repeated stubbornly. 'And I can't believe that you would want to sully the de Salvatore name by marrying one of the notorious Balfour sisters either!'

'It would not have been my first choice, no,' Luc acknowledged wryly.

'Or your last!' Annie guessed easily.

'It *is* my last,' he drawled. 'And I have no doubt that such a marriage will prove to have some compensations,' he added.

Annie felt the warm colour enter her cheeks at his deliberately provocative tone. 'I'm not marrying any man, let alone sharing his bed, when I'm not in love with him,' she insisted.

Luc's gaze narrowed as he heard the vehement determination in her tone. Every inch of her was tensed as if for a fight. From the fiery lights in that thick chestnut-coloured hair, and the tension in her body, to the bareness of her toes now curled into the carpet as if ready to spring into action if necessary.

She really was very beautiful.

A beautiful woman possessed of an inner fire that had already succeeded in melting Luc's own coolness more than once.

Even now Luc felt a stirring, a hardening, of his thighs as he recalled their time together earlier today, of the way she had been prepared to fight him then too. Before passion had replaced her anger...

'You did not seem to find the idea of sharing my bed so distasteful this afternoon,' he pointed out as he allowed his gaze to deliberately move down to the firm thrust of her breasts. Breasts that were full and pouting, and obviously unconfined beneath that fitted T-shirt, the tips becoming engorged with arousal even as Luc looked at them.

Annie resisted the urge to cross her arms over that betraying hardening of her nipples. What was it about this man in particular that made her respond this way? Whatever it was, Annie couldn't allow it—wouldn't allow it!—to affect her resolve not to give in to Luc's demands.

She shook her head. 'A marriage that isn't based on love will ultimately fail. One or both of us is sure to one day meet someone we can love, and then we would have to go through the messy process of a divorce.'

Luc raised dark brows. 'You speak as if from experience...'

Had she?

Yes, of course she had!

Annie's mother and father had only married each other because Oscar had been left with three very young daughters following the death of his first wife. Tilly, as nanny to those three little girls, had been the obvious choice to become Oscar's second wife. And because Tilly liked and respected Oscar, and already loved his three young daughters to distraction, she had accepted his marriage proposal. Only to then meet Victor, the man she had fallen instantly in love with, four years and three daughters of her own later.

The fact that Tilly and Oscar's separation and divorce had been amicable, that they remained close friends, hadn't made the experience of having parents who were divorced any less traumatic for Annie.

Strangely, Annie had never admitted that before, even to herself.

She was only doing so now because she had no intention of putting Oliver through that same heartbreak!

'The break-up of your own parents' marriage might have something to do with that?' Luc guessed with that shrewdness that could be so unnerving.

Everything about this man was unnerving, Annie acknowledged frustratedly. From the cold chill of his ruthlessness, to the way that just looking at him made her heart beat faster and her breath catch in her throat!

The fact that, in spite of everything, she was still physically attracted to Luc was no basis for a marriage between them either, she told herself firmly.

'Being at the centre of a divorce, even an amicable one, is never good for the children,' she said bluntly.

'Then it is as well that my family does not believe in divorce,' Luc said.

'I don't believe in marriages of convenience either.' Annie stubbornly stood her ground. 'That results in a stalemate, I believe, Luc!'

Her father, following the scandal that had occurred at the 100th Balfour Charity Ball, had lectured all of his daughters on the necessity of restoring some pride and dignity back into the Balfour name. In an effort to instil his determination into his more rebellious daughters, he had dragged out an ancient family manuscript outlining the code of honour by which the Balfours had once lived. Antiquated that code may have been, but one of them had remained fixed in Annie's mind ever since: *A Balfour should be frightened of nothing. Face your fears with courage and they will lead to further self-discovery.*

Meeting Oliver's father again had always been Annie's biggest fear!

An occurrence that had already led her to one piece of surprising self-discovery—she had never before realised how much she had been affected by the heartache of growing up with parents who were divorced....

But she realised it now, and that realisation made her more determined than ever that Oliver's childhood would not be blighted by his parents suffering the same fate.

'Perhaps,' Luc answered her softly now.

Despite her own resolve, Annie wasn't sure she particularly cared for that determined glint in Luc's coal-black eyes. She liked it even less when that dark gaze again moved slowly over the curves of her body to once again create a tingling in her breasts and that rush of heat between her thighs.

A heat that suffused all of Annie's body, making her skin ultra sensitive, and her close-fitting jeans and T-shirt suddenly feel uncomfortably tight...

She gave a self-disgusted sigh at this response to just having Luc's gaze upon her body. 'I need to go outside for some air,' she announced. She didn't wait for Luc's response but turned on her heel to move across the room, opening the door to the balcony and stepping outside to breathe in the fresh, clean—sobering!—air.

Luc remained unmoving for several seconds after she had gone outside.

He had no doubts that she meant it when she said she wouldn't marry him. Luc's own resolve that such a marriage *would* take place was also unshakeable. Oliver Balfour was his son, and Anna Balfour was the mother of that son. There was no question, absolutely no doubt in Luc's mind, that she would become his wife.

Luc stepped outside to cross the balcony to where she stood against the balustrade looking out at the evening beauty of Lake Garda. Or giving the appearance of looking across Lake Garda; the defensive stiffening of her shoulders told him that she was completely aware of him standing directly behind her.

Because she feared him?

Or was her tension for another reason completely?

Luc stepped forward, his body mere centimetres away from hers as his hands moved either side of her to rest lightly on the balustrade and hold her trapped within his encircling arms. 'Your hair smells of flowers and sunshine,' he murmured as he breathed in her heady perfume—flowers, sunshine and an underlying musk of sensuality.

Her throat moved convulsively before she answered him. 'I think you'll find that it's the flowers in the bowers hanging off the balcony that you can smell.'

Luc laughed softly. 'Allow me a little poetic licence.'

Every part of Annie was tinglingly aware of every part of Luc. The warmth of his breath against her exposed throat. The powerful heat of his body as he stepped even closer. The hardness of his arousal as it pressed intimately against her bottom…

'What are you doing, Luc?' she breathed huskily even as her throat arched and she felt the warm rasp of his tongue against the heat of her skin.

'Demonstrating one of those compensations,' he murmured as he nibbled the lobe of her ear.

Annie had been out on several dates the past three years. She had even liked some of those men enough to go out on second and third dates with them. But none of those men had ever made her want to throw off all her clothes and offer herself to him in the way that Luc did, both in the lift earlier and again now.

'I'm not going to marry you, Luc,' she managed to tell him breathlessly.

'No?' His hands moved up to cup her breasts, the soft pads of both his thumbs caressingly lightly over the swollen tips of her breasts.

'No.' Annie gasped as heat coursed from her breasts down into her thighs.

'Do you not remember how it was between us, Annie?' He moved the hardness of his erection against her bottom. 'How we couldn't get enough of each other that night?'

Yes, of course Annie remembered! It was those memories of being with Luc, more than anything else, that had prevented her from being able to enter into another relationship with someone else!

Meeting Luc in the way she had, daring to spend that single wild and passionate night with him, had been completely out of character for Annie. Until that night she had always been the most quiet and practical one, preferring to spend her time at Balfour Manor with Tilly rather than flitting from party to party as two of her older sisters did.

Her emotions once she realised she was pregnant had been a tangle of contradiction. Part of her had been terrified at the thought of having a baby. Another part of her had been thrilled at the thought of the child growing inside her.

Luc's child.

Not Luca de Salvatore's.

After all, she didn't even know Luca de Salvatore.

Except that she seemed to respond to him as readily as she had Luc all those years ago…

Annie's mouth tightened. 'Before you did your disappearing act the following day, you mean?'

'There was a good reason for that—'

'I'm sure there was!' she scorned as she recalled the humiliation of sitting in a restaurant the evening following their night together, waiting for a Luc who had never arrived. She twisted out of his restraining arms now to put some distance between them. '*I* remembered that night, Luc—you're the one that didn't,' she reminded him tensely.

Luc's mouth thinned, and his hands clenched at his sides in frustration.

No, to his shame, he hadn't initially remembered spending that night with this beautiful young woman. But there really *was* an explanation for that. Maybe not an acceptable one to the woman who had given birth to and brought up his son alone, but it was an explanation, nonetheless.

A shameful explanation that had been the driving force behind all of Luc's thoughts and actions this past four and a half years…

Through his arrogance he had brought the de Salvatore business empire to its knees. And then, instead of remaining in Rome to help his father try to repair the damage he had done, Luc had taken himself off to enjoy the Italian ski slopes. Had closed his mind to the mistakes he had made by indulging in a frenzy of pleasure that had culminated in him taking Anna Balfour to his bed.

What Luc hadn't known, hadn't realised until the following morning, was that while he had been busy enjoying himself, his father had suffered a heart attack as a consequence of Luc's mismanagement, and was in hospital fighting for his life.

He had seen the news of his father's collapse in a newspaper, of all places!

Having arranged to meet Annie later that day, Luc had instead ended his holiday abruptly and returned to Rome to be at his father's bedside.

How could he possibly have known—how could he have guessed?—that by doing so he had abandoned Annie to the fate of giving birth to their son alone?

Luc sighed. 'I am no longer the self-centred young man I was four and a half years ago.'

Annie gave a rueful acknowledgement of her head at the truth of that. 'Luckily, I'm not as naively trusting as I was then either,' she assured him drily.

His mouth twisted. 'Have any of the Balfour sisters ever been "naively trusting"?'

Annie drew in a sharp breath. 'I really don't believe we're going to achieve anything by insulting each other.'

'No,' he acknowledged, that nerve once again pulsing in his tightly clenched jaw. 'Nevertheless, we *are* going to be married, Anna,' he stated evenly.

Annie gave him a pityingly look. 'It's a long time since anyone said no to you, isn't it, Luc?'

He gave a humourless smile. 'I do not remember anyone ever doing so.'

'I just did,' she pointed out.

'Yes.' He nodded slowly, those dark eyes glittering in the moonlight. 'But you do so in the knowledge that I will fight for my son if necessary.'

Of course Annie knew that Luc wasn't about to just

walk away from Oliver because she refused to marry him. She doubted that the man who stood before her, so hard, so ruthlessly intractable, had ever walked away from a fight. He certainly wasn't about to walk away from his own son!

Annie swallowed hard. 'The media will eat us alive if we fight over Oliver in a court of law,' she said heavily.

Luc shrugged. 'That is your choice.'

Annie looked at him searchingly, knowing by the hard challenge she could read in Luc's expression that he wasn't going to back down.

But the alternative to the horror of a court battle was marriage. To Luca de Salvatore. A Luca de Salvatore who was no more in love with Annie than she was with him.

She couldn't do it!

Luc easily read the determined resolve in her face as she obviously came to her decision. A decision, he had no doubt, that would result in the two of them facing each other across a courtroom as they fought, by any means possible, for custody of their son. A very public and bloody battle that would no doubt also end with them hating each other as they were left with no choice but to rip each other's characters and past behaviour to shreds.

'You would be very foolish to even contemplate fighting me in that way, Anna,' he warned softly.

Her pointed chin rose to that challenge. 'With my own parents' broken marriage as an example, I would be even more foolish to contemplate marrying a man I don't love and who doesn't love me!'

'Just because your father was not successful in keeping

your mother contented in their marriage bed does not mean that I would fail to keep you happy in the same way!' Luc stated arrogantly.

Anna's cheeks coloured. 'My father kept my mother contented enough for her to produce three daughters in three years!'

Luc regarded her coldly. 'Would you not like more children of your own, Anna? Or do you feel you have already done your duty by producing a son?'

'Of course I would like more children,' she snapped. 'Just not with a man I don't love!'

Luc gave a derisive snort. 'I am surprised, considering your own childhood, to hear that you still believe in this elusive emotion called love.'

She looked rueful. 'Just because my parents never loved each other in that romantic way doesn't mean that they didn't both find love, true love, with other people.'

Luc scowled darkly. 'And you fear, if we were to marry for Oliver's sake, the same thing might happen to one or both of us some time in the future?'

Did Annie fear that?

Or was her biggest fear, if she were to agree to marry Luc, that it might be *him* that she fell in love with? While he continued to feel nothing more than contempt for *Anna Balfour*, as he continued to call her.

She was back to that challenging Balfour code again: *Face your fears with courage and they will lead to further self-discovery.*

What if it should turn out that Annie's biggest fear, the most momentous self-discovery she made, was that the reason she had never fallen in love with any

of the men she had dated the past three years was
because she had never been able to get over that night
she had spent with Luc?

CHAPTER SIX

ANNIE repressed a shiver just at the thought of her emotions being completely at the mercy of Luca de Salvatore's legendary ruthlessness. 'In your case?' she bit out. 'Somehow I doubt that very much!'

Luc's eyes narrowed ominously. 'You believe me incapable of feeling love for another person?'

She grimaced. 'I believe Luca de Salvatore to be capable of dismissing any emotion that might result in him feeling in the least vulnerable.'

How well she already knew him, Luc thought. As far as he was concerned, love for one's family, especially one's children, was permissible. But to feel love for a woman was to leave oneself totally vulnerable.

For any man to ever fall in love with one of the capricious and fickle Balfour sisters would be the height of foolishness!

To feel desire for one, however, was another matter entirely...

He looked at her quizzically. 'And what of the man you met four and a half years ago? Do you believe him to be incapable of emotion too?'

Annie looked at Luc for some seconds. The hard glitter of his eyes. That thinned mouth. The inflexibility of his jaw. 'They're one and the same man,' she finally stated flatly.

'You did not seem to think so once,' he said.

Annie shrugged. 'I was young and easily impressed.'

'And four short years later you have succeeded in eliminating such childish illusions?' Luc taunted.

'Having a baby when you're unmarried and alone will do that to you every time,' Annie said tightly.

He stiffened. 'You chose—'

'I didn't *choose* anything, Luc!' Annie cried. 'How could I have done anything else but what I did when I had no idea who you were? And if you think, just because I'm one of the infamous Balfour sisters, that it was easy telling my parents I was pregnant, then I suggest you think again!' she snapped angrily as Luc continued to look at her with that chilling intensity. 'It was—' She broke off, shaking her head slightly as she recalled that awful evening when she'd had to get her father and mother together at Balfour Manor and tell them she was three months pregnant.

Oscar had been furious, demanding to know the name of the father—with the obvious intention of beating the man to within an inch of his life for daring to get one of his daughters pregnant! He had become angrier still when Annie had tearfully refused to—because she couldn't—tell him the father's name.

As usual, it had been left to Tilly to calm the situation, as she first comforted Annie and then soothed Oscar's angry protestations, pointing out the futility of Oscar knowing the name of the father of Annie's baby when Annie obviously wanted nothing more to do with him.

Not quite true, of course; Annie had been left with no choice when Luc had disappeared so abruptly that day. But at least the abruptness of his departure from the Italian ski slopes, as well as from her life, had shown Annie only too clearly that as far as Luc was concerned that one night together had been enough. Pride, more than anything else, had dictated that Annie didn't try to find Luc just because she had realised she was pregnant.

She had always been sensible. Practical. For her to then be the daughter who ended up alone and pregnant had been mortifying!

'Some of my sisters may sometimes behave outrageously, but—' Annie shook her head. 'My parents never said so, never voiced any recriminations, in fact, but I know that I must have disappointed them terribly when I became pregnant,' Annie acknowledged heavily.

Luc could see the pain of that admission in the darkness of her eyes and the pallor of her cheeks.

Something Luc understood only too well when he had let his own father down so badly himself. It wasn't the same thing, of course, but—

'You did not consider…terminating the pregnancy?'

'Of course not!' That fire returned to Annie's eyes. 'And my parents didn't suggest it either, if that was going to be your next question,' she said. 'The Balfour family may make the newspaper headlines on a regular basis, but I don't think anyone can ever accuse us of running away from our responsibilities.'

No, Luc knew he certainly could not accuse her of doing that.

'You—' He broke off as a knock sounded on the outer door of the hotel suite.

'That's probably room service with my dinner,' Annie realised. 'You're more than welcome to share my club sandwich if you haven't already eaten,' she offered as she moved lightly across the balcony and back into the suite. The food would probably choke her after this conversation with Luc anyway!

What followed, after Luc's earlier accusations and threats, was slightly surreal as far as Annie was concerned.

Whoever would have imagined that the two of them would be able to sit down together and make polite—if slightly stilted—conversation?

Annie certainly wouldn't have thought it possible, but that's exactly what they did as they waited for the waiter to return with a second club sandwich for Luc. That conversation became less general and more personal once the waiter left them alone a second time.

'Have you attended one of these management conferences before?' Luc asked.

'No. Daddy just decided that it was time that I did.' She had no intention of telling Luc of her father's ridiculous decision to send all of his daughters out into the world to seek their destiny.

'Really?' Luc frowned across at her. 'So you did not want to come to Italy?'

'Not particularly.'

'Possibly because it was where we met?' Luc guessed astutely.

Annie looked him straight in the eye. 'Italy is a big place, Luc.'

'Obviously not big enough!' he drawled drily.

'Obviously not.' She grimaced. 'But even so, you have to admit, the chances of us meeting again were pretty remote.'

'And yet it happened.'

'Pure fluke,' Annie stated.

'Was it?'

'Exactly what are you implying?' Annie eyed him warily. 'That I deliberately came back to Italy with the intention of finally seeking you out?'

He raised dark brows over those remorseless black eyes. 'Did you?'

'Absolutely not,' she denied, deeply resenting the fact that he had thought she might have done so. 'I work for my father, Luc, and as such, I have to go where he tells me to go.'

He considered her closely. 'But you said you do not like working for your father?'

Liking didn't come into it; it had simply been the easiest and most convenient thing for Annie to do to earn a living once she considered that Oliver was old enough to be left with her mother for a few hours every day.

Annie eyed Luc defensively. 'Not particularly, no. But that doesn't mean I'm not good at what I do.'

'No?'

'No,' Annie said. 'A couple of years ago I helped my mother put her small cookery business on a financially viable footing—'

'A cottage industry does not compare to one of international proportions—'

'I've only been here twenty-four hours, Luc, but already I can tell you that this hotel doesn't have enough receptionists. I had to wait ten minutes yesterday in order to book in. The health club should open earlier than seven-thirty in the morning. There aren't enough restaurants for the number of guests. A bar actually on the beach would add to the guests' comfort and enjoyment. And that's only after a cursory observation,' Annie added challengingly. 'I'm sure I could find more room for improvement if I were to go into it more thoroughly.'

Luc sat back to look at her in reluctant admiration. 'You have inherited your father's business acumen, I see.'

'So it would seem, yes,' Annie said a little smugly.

'Perhaps I should consider hiring you myself?'

'You couldn't afford me!'

Luc's admiration turned to amusement. Certainly no one could accuse Anna Balfour of a lack of self-confidence!

He sobered. 'The offer was actually a serious one, Anna, in the event you might wish to continue working after we are married.'

'Oh, please, not that again!' She pushed her plate of food away almost untouched before standing, those deep blue eyes glittering angrily as she looked down at Luc. 'I have no intention of marrying you. Not now. Not ever,' she added with finality.

Luc had never before met a woman as determined to thwart him as Anna Balfour—or Annie Balfour, as she preferred to be called.

Or one apparently so unaware of her own sensual allure...

The red lights in her chestnut-coloured hair seemed all the deeper beneath the overhead light. Her eyes as deep and clear a blue as the lake outside. Her complexion a perfect cream. The bow of her lips full and sensuous.

It was also impossible to ignore the allure of her curvaceous body—as he had discovered earlier those full breasts definitely were completely bare beneath her T-shirt, her waist flat above the low waistband of her jeans. As for the way that denim hugged the contours of her rounded bottom…

Luc felt a tightening of his thighs just looking at her! And the way she smelled was delicious. There was that floral perfume, of course, but beneath that, elusive but still discernable, was a hint of heat, of sexual arousal, that touched a part of Luc he had long thought subdued.

'Do not be too quick to reject the idea, Annie,' he murmured throatily as he slowly stood.

Annie's eyes widened as Luc now stood towering over her. 'We aren't back to those compensations again, are we?' She tried to inject scorn into her tone, but even to her own ears she sounded nervous rather than scornful!

That nervousness increased as Luc lifted a hand to gently cup one side of her face, those fingers seeming to burn where they touched. 'You are a very beautiful woman, Annie.'

Just the way Luc said her name, huskily, with a hint of sensual persuasion, was enough to set alarm bells ringing in her head. 'I'm also a Balfour,' she reminded him tartly as she stood her ground in a determined effort to keep Luc from seeing how much his touch affected her.

Luc's mouth quirked. 'That would no longer be true if you married me. Then you would become Anna de Salvatore.' Strange how right that sounded.

She gave a rueful shake of her head. 'Being a Balfour is a state of mind, not just a name,' she told him.

'Not all of your sisters are considered wild and unruly,' Luc pointed out.

Annie gave a short laugh. 'I'm sure they would be thrilled to hear it!'

His eyes narrowed. 'It was merely an observation, not a personal opinion.'

Annie glared at him. 'I may have become one of those wilder Balfour sisters if I hadn't had Oliver to think of.'

Luc's nostrils flared. 'Believe me, I need no reminder that my behaviour changed the course of your life.'

Maybe not, but Annie certainly did!

In fact, she needed every defence she could dredge up in order to fight against the sensual spell Luc's close proximity was weaving around her already battered emotions.

'Don't do that!' she muttered achingly as Luc raised a hand and ran his thumb across her slightly parted lips.

'Why not?' he asked. 'Does your physical attraction to me bother you?'

'Does your physical attraction to me bother you?' she came back challengingly.

'At this moment?' he considered gruffly. 'No.'

Annie groaned as the softness of his thumb once again swept across the sensitivity of her bottom lip before dipping into the moist heat beneath. 'Luc!'

'Annie?' he replied hoarsely even as his head lowered and his lips replaced that caressing thumb.

No man should possess such a wickedly sensual mouth. Or hands that felt so deliciously hot as they cupped her bottom to pull her in tight against his hard body. A hard body that moulded so perfectly to her softness that she could already feel the pulsing heat of his arousal…

An arousal that was all the more heady to Annie's already inflamed senses because it was Luca de Salvatore, and not Luc, who felt it. A man well-known for his cold ruthlessness, both in business and his personal relationships.

Luc was anything but cold at this moment, his mouth hot and demanding against Annie's, the sweep of his tongue parting her lips even further to thrust into the warm cavern beneath. He instinctively deepened that kiss as Annie's hands moved caressingly across the hardness of his chest before her fingers reached up and clasped his shoulders.

His mouth devoured, beckoned, drawing her tongue into a duel with his, those hard thrusts enticing Annie into returning the caress.

Luc growled low in his throat as he felt that first tentative response, and then captured her tongue inside his mouth before she could withdraw it, needing to take her into him, and to be a part of her.

He moved one of his hands to support the back of her head as their kisses became wilder, more demanding, his fingers becoming entangled in that chestnut-coloured richness as his lips and tongue continued to taste her. His other hand moved to skim lightly over the flatness of her stomach, ribs and finally against the underside of her breast.

Annie wrenched her mouth from Luc's to purr low in her throat as he repeated that caress, feeling her breast swell and harden beneath his touch, her nipples becoming twin aching point of pleasure. Of aching, decadent need...

Her neck arched instinctively as Luc's clever mouth sought out the hollows of her throat, the movement thrusting her breasts forward. Annie groaned, burning hotly between her thighs as Luc's hand cupped a breast to capture one aching nipple between his thumb and finger, squeezing lightly, pleasurably.

She moved restlessly against Luc in an effort to ease that pulsing ache, rubbing rhythmically against the hardness of his erection as it throbbed and swelled with the same need. She was pulled even closer still as Luc hooked a hand beneath her denim-clad knee to raise her leg and lift her up into him so that the full thrust of his arousal touched the sensitive place between her thighs.

But it wasn't enough. Would never be enough. Annie needed, oh, God, she needed—

'Tell me what you want!' Luc rasped gruffly against Annie's throat. 'Tell me, Annie!' he demanded as she continued to move restlessly against him.

Until Luc answered her Annie hadn't even been aware that she had spoken out loud! 'I—' She broke off in a gasp as one of Luc's hands cupped her between her legs.

She needed Luc inside her. Deep, deep inside her, until she had no idea where she ended and Luc began…

'Tell me, Annie!' Luc insisted again as he looked down at her fiercely, the palm of his hand moving rhythmically against her as he felt her heat through the material of her jeans. 'Say it, Annie. Tell me what you need.'

She moistened lips swollen from his kisses, those blue eyes slightly dazed as she looked up at him. 'I want—' She cried low in her throat as Luc pressed harder, deeper, between her thighs even as he lowered his head and placed his lips about the hard tip of her breast, drawing that fullness into the heated wetness of his mouth, his tongue rasping, his teeth gently biting. 'Oh!' she gasped weakly.

'Say it!' Luc demanded relentlessly.

'You're driving me crazy, Luc!' she cried achingly, eyes fever bright with need.

Luc pressed his fingers into her. 'Tell me you want me, Annie. Say it!' he said hoarsely.

'I—' She whimpered her longing as Luc ceased his caresses. 'Don't stop, Luc. For God's sake, don't stop…'

His eyes blazed as he cupped his hands beneath her bottom and lifted her completely off the floor. Her hands clung to his shoulders, her legs curved around his waist, as he carried her to the sofa.

Annie found herself looking down at Luc as he sat, her legs straddling his thighs, and her knees on the cushions of the sofa on either side of him. This position pressed his hardness even more intimately against that aching throb between her legs.

The darkness of Luc's gaze held hers captive as he peeled her T-shirt up and over the fullness of her breasts, his gaze becoming even hungrier as he looked down at those soft and creamy swells tipped with nipples that were swollen and rose coloured.

Annie felt the heat course through her body as Luc continued to look at her breasts, tongue flicking across his lips, moistening them, causing her breasts to tingle even more as she quivered in anticipation of feeling those lips against her bared flesh.

She watched, fascinated, as Luc slowly lowered his head, the warmth of his breath moving lightly over her even as his tongue rasped briefly—too briefly!—against one aching nipple.

Annie arched into that caress as Luc's mouth continued that slow leisurely torture of her breast before transferring his attention to its twin. 'Don't tease me!' she groaned, her hands moving up, fingers becoming entangled in the dark thickness of Luc's hair as she pulled him harder against her, that groan turning to an aching moan as Luc took her deeply into the heat of his mouth and his fingers moved to the fastening on her jeans before sliding down beneath the lace of her panties.

Annie almost sobbed with pleasure as she undulated against the skilful fingers that found and then caressed the swollen nub nestled there. Those caresses becoming faster, harder, as Annie rushed towards a climax so fierce, so mind-numbingly glorious, that when it finally came to an end she could only collapse weakly against Luc's shoulder as she fought for breath.

Luc's own breathing was deep and ragged as he held her against him, satisfied for the moment with the knowledge that he had given Annie pleasure. He didn't need to know that pleasure himself when he could still feel how she trembled and quivered so delightfully in his arms.

Annie obviously had other ideas as she moved to sit up and pull up his polo shirt, sitting back slightly as she rolled the shirt up his body and over his head before casting it aside. Her concentration was total as the slenderness of her hands touched his much darker flesh; her fingers caressed the muscled hardness, manicured nails scraping teasingly across the hardened nubs nestled amongst the light dusting of dark hair that covered Luc's chest.

Luc sucked his breath in sharply when those fingers moved lower still, unfastening the button on his own jeans, Annie's gaze boldly holding his now as she moved off him to kneel on the cushion beside him. She slowly slid the zip down, pushing his jeans and black boxers

FREE Merchandise is 'in the Cards' for you!

Dear Reader,

We're giving away FREE MERCHANDISE!

Seriously, we'd like to reward you for reading this novel by giving you **FREE MERCHANDISE** worth over **$20**. And no purchase is necessary!

You see the Jack of Hearts sticker above? Paste that sticker in the box on the Free Merchandise Voucher inside. Return the Voucher promptly...and we'll send you valuable Free Merchandise!

Thanks again for reading one of our novels—and enjoy your Free Merchandise with our compliments!

Pam Powers

Pam Powers

P.S. Look inside to see what Free Merchandise is **"in the cards"** for you!

We'd like to send you two free books to introduce you to the Harlequin Presents® series. These books are worth over $10, but they are yours to keep absolutely FREE! We'll even send you 2 wonderful surprise gifts. You can't lose!

REMEMBER: Your Free Merchandise, consisting of **2 Free Books** and **2 Free Gifts**, is worth over $20.00! No purchase is necessary, so please send for your Free Merchandise today.

Plus TWO FREE GIFTS!

We'll also send you two wonderful FREE GIFTS (worth about $10), in addition to your 2 Free Harlequin Presents® books!

Order online at:
www.ReaderService.com

YOUR FREE MERCHANDISE INCLUDES...

2 FREE Harlequin Presents® Books

AND 2 FREE Mystery Gifts

FREE MERCHANDISE VOUCHER

2 FREE BOOKS
and
2 FREE GIFTS

Please send my Free Merchandise, consisting of
2 Free Books and **2 Free Mystery Gifts**.
I understand that I am under no obligation to buy
anything, as explained on the back of this card.

*About how many NEW paperback fiction books
have you purchased in the past 3 months?*

☐ 0-2   ☐ 3-6   ☐ 7 or more
  E9HY   E9JC   E9JN

☐ I prefer the regular-print edition   ☐ I prefer the larger-print edition
  106/306 HDL   **176/376 HDL**

Please Print

FIRST NAME

LAST NAME

ADDRESS

APT.#   CITY

STATE/PROV.   ZIP/POSTAL CODE

NO PURCHASE NECESSARY!

▲ If offer card is missing write to: The Reader Service, P.O. Box 1867, Buffalo, NY 14240-1867 or visit www.ReaderService.com ▲

BUSINESS REPLY MAIL
FIRST-CLASS MAIL   PERMIT NO. 717   BUFFALO, NY

POSTAGE WILL BE PAID BY ADDRESSEE

THE READER SERVICE
PO BOX 1867
BUFFALO NY 14240-9952

NO POSTAGE
NECESSARY
IF MAILED
IN THE
UNITED STATES

aside before curling her fingers about his throbbing hardness.

Luc groaned as he allowed his head to fall back against the sofa, eyes closed as he revelled in the sensation of having Annie's fingers wrapped around him. Fingers that slowly moved along the swollen length of him, from base to tip, causing him to harden even further.

Annie was emboldened, empowered, as she felt as well as saw this physical evidence of the depth of Luc's arousal. Her gaze held his once again as her fingers curled firmly about him before she lowered her head and took him into the heat of her mouth.

She saw his eyes widen even as he tensed beneath the unexpected intimacy and his hands moved to grip her shoulders tightly, with the obvious intention of pushing her away from him.

Annie refused to budge, shrugging off those restraining hands as she paused to lick along the length of him before once again sucking him deeply into her mouth.

He tasted as sweet and warm as honey, of hot pleasure and even hotter sex, the urgent increasing thrum beneath her mouth and fingers telling her how close Luc was to release. She drew him in deeper still as Luc's hands became entangled in her hair, no longer pushing her away but holding her in place as he couldn't seem to stop himself from thrusting into the heated wetness of her mouth.

Luc felt his normal control slipping, evaporating, as he found himself aware only of Annie, of the caress of her lips, tongue and fingers as they moved against his hard and fevered flesh.

He became rock hard as he felt himself poised on the

very edge of release—and how he wanted, craved, that release! But—

'No!' Luc's fingers tightened in Annie's hair and he carefully pulled her up and away from him before standing. He moved right across the room, his back turned towards her as he refastened his jeans, and then ran a hand through the dark thickness of his hair as he drew deep, controlling breaths into his starved and aching lungs.

Annie sat back on her heels to look across at Luc dazedly, too stunned for several seconds to understand, let alone accept, that Luc had brought an end to their lovemaking.

Arousing Luc had made her ache all over again. Everywhere. And seconds ago Luc had ached and throbbed with that same need.

The uncompromising rigidity of the muscled back and shoulders he kept turned firmly towards her told her that was no longer the case.

Minutes ago Annie had almost ripped Luc's polo shirt from his body in her burning need to touch him, to feel the heat of his naked skin beneath her caressing hands. All of his heat.

Her cheeks flamed as she remembered how she had hurriedly unfastened Luc's jeans in her need to touch him more intimately still. To taste him.

To touch and taste Luca de Salvatore intimately!

Dear heaven above, what had she just done…?

CHAPTER SEVEN

Luc was disgusted with himself as he kept his back firmly turned towards Annie.

It had been his intention to kiss her, to touch her, in order to show her they were still physically attracted to each other, if nothing else.

Instead Luc had only succeeded in proving that Anna Balfour was a danger to the rigid self-control he had exerted over his emotions—all his emotions—for the past four years.

If he needed food, then he ate. If he required liquid, then he drank. And if he needed physical release, then he took a woman to his bed. Coldly. Calculatedly.

The pleasure he had just received in kissing and touching Annie, in having her kiss and touch him in return, had not been in the least cold or calculated. Instead she had reached him, pierced the armour he kept about his emotions, driven him to an excess of physical pleasure, in a way no other woman had for years. Since Luc had last made love to her, in fact!

He drew in several harsh, controlling breaths before turning to face her, his jaw tightening as he took in the evidence of their lovemaking in the tousled wildness of her hair and the swollen fullness of her lips. Lips that minutes ago had been wrapped around—

'Do you still dismiss those "compensations" so hastily?' he asked as he picked up his polo shirt and pulled it back over the nakedness of his torso.

Annie was glad she had taken advantage of Luc's few minutes of distraction to straighten her own clothing as she saw the hardness of his expression and those dark, uncompromising eyes.

'What can I say, Luc—you're still an accomplished lover.' She shrugged. 'No doubt you've had plenty of opportunities to practise your technique over the years.'

His jaw tightened at the deliberate insult. 'As have you,' he pointed out coldly.

Annie almost laughed at the ridiculousness of that accusation when she hadn't so much as thought about a man in that way since Luc. Except there was nothing in the least funny about this situation.

To say that she was stunned by her response to him was an understatement!

Just as the way she had touched him, caressed him, had been purely instinctive. Annie had no other experience on which to draw except that time with him more than four years ago.

Luc frowned fiercely. 'Do you have someone in your life at the moment?'

Only Luc himself! 'Do you?' She evaded the question by slamming it straight back at him.

'I have…the occasional woman in my bed,' he revealed slowly. 'But not recently,' he added tightly.

'OK, comparing past or present lovers isn't conducive to this conversation.' Not when Annie had felt a shaft of jealousy course through her at Luc's admission.

'There will be no other lovers for either of us once you are my wife—'

'Are you hearing impaired, Luc?' Annie cut in sharply as she stood. 'I've told you numerous times now that I'm *not* going to *be* your wife.'

'You have another solution to this situation?'

Her solution was that Luc disappear out of her life as completely as he had re-entered it! A solution he had unfortunately already rejected.

'None that seem to be acceptable to you, no. But—'

'There can be no buts, Anna,' Luc growled. 'Either we marry or we commence a legal battle over Oliver. A battle that will no doubt become a very public one, considering who we are. After the recent scandal concerning the illegitimacy of one of your sisters, how do you think your father will react to a custody battle over his grandson?' he added challengingly.

Annie gave a pained gasp. 'You bastard!'

'On the contrary, my own legitimacy has never been in question,' Luc drawled.

She glared at him. 'Only your son's!'

Luc's eyes glittered as black as coal. 'Yes.'

Annie frowned her frustration. A month ago she would have had no hesitation in telling Luc to do his worst. Before the scandal at the Balfour Charity Ball. Before, as Luc so rightly pointed out, the legitimacy of one of Oscar's own daughters had been brought into question.

Could the timing of this have been any worse?

She clenched her fists in utter frustration. 'We're going round and round in ever-decreasing circles with this conversation, Luc.'

His mouth firmed. 'That will cease once you stop fighting the inevitable.'

'There's nothing in the least *inevitable* about your demand that I marry you!' Annie exclaimed.

'No?'

Was it really inevitable that she agree to marry Luc? He seemed to think that it was.

So what if he did think that? Damn it, she may be one of the less aggressive Balfour sisters, but she was still a Balfour, and as such she did not intend allowing *anyone* to bully her into doing something she didn't want to do.

'Our union promises to be a stormy one,' Luc murmured ruefully as Annie's expression easily gave away her thoughts. The doubts, quickly followed by a renewed determination more than equal to his own forceful nature.

Her eyes flashed a deep, sapphire blue. 'If you succeed in forcing me to marry you, Luc, then I promise you I will make it my ambition to ensure that your own life becomes a living hell!'

Luc had no doubts that they would have disagreements once they were married. But his very nature demanded that he could never be content with a woman who simply bowed to his dictates, and Annie Balfour had already shown that she had no intention of doing that.

He smiled wickedly. 'I will look forward to seeing you try.'

'I wouldn't if I were you,' she warned.

Luc gave an unconcerned shrug. 'So we are in agreement, then, that our marriage—'

'We are in agreement on *nothing*!' Annie interrupted

hotly. 'And until we are, I don't think it's a good idea for you to meet Oliver—'

'Agreed.'

'—and upset him with this…this dissention between the two of us. It will only confuse him—'

'I said I agree, Annie.'

'—and that can't be good for any of us. *What* did you say?' Annie looked across at him in confusion.

'I said I agree, Annie,' he repeated patiently. 'It is not my intention to confuse or upset Oliver either.'

'Oh.' Annie felt a little like a deflated balloon. 'So we're agreed that I will go back to England on Monday, somehow try to explain the situation to Oliver, and then—'

'No, that is not what I said at all.' Luc gave a brief smile.

She sighed. 'You aren't making any sense, Luc.'

'I believe, if you listen closely to what I am saying, you will find I am making complete sense,' Luc assured her drily. 'Neither of us will return to England to be with Oliver until the situation between us has been resolved.'

Much as Luc longed to see Oliver, to see his son for the first time, he appreciated that to do so while he and Annie were still at loggerheads over their future would not be beneficial to any of them. Least of all Oliver.

The little boy had spent the first few years of his young life living happily with his mother and grandmother. No doubt with lots of visits from his grandfather and his many aunts. As such, Luc knew that his own introduction into Oliver's life had to be done in a way that would be acceptable to the little boy. More importantly, it would be far better for Oliver if his mother and father could at least have a conversation without resorting to argument or insult!

'You mean once I've resigned myself to marrying you?' Annie said with patent disgust.

Luc raised dark, arrogant brows. 'Exactly.'

She gave a derisive snort. 'You're tenacious, I'll give you that.'

'As are you,' he murmured appreciatively.

Her eyes narrowed. 'So what's the plan, Luc? We remain here and continue arguing the point until one of us—namely me—sees reason?'

He grimaced. 'Staying on at the hotel would not be practical when my business here is complete and you have arrangements to leave here on Monday.'

'So what are you suggesting?' She eyed him warily.

'I had originally planned to spend several days at the de Salvatore vineyard near Venice once I left here. If you were to come with me—'

'You want me to come to Venice with you?' Annie gasped. Venice was supposed to be one of the most romantic cities in the world, wasn't it?

'The de Salvatore vineyards are in the hills above Venice,' Luc corrected.

Venice itself, or the hills above the city, what did it really matter when Annie would be alone there with Luca de Salvatore! When this evening had already shown her how dangerous it was for her to be alone with him *anywhere*!

She shook her head. 'I don't—'

'The alternative is for me to accompany you back to England as originally suggested,' Luc pointed out coolly.

One look at the utter determination on Luc's face was enough to tell Annie that he meant the threat.

As if she had ever doubted it!

'What if, after these several days, we still haven't managed to find a compromise over Oliver's future?' she challenged.

Those black eyes were cold and merciless. 'I am confident that we will have done so.'

Annie felt as if she were up to her neck in quicksand. As if the whole of the world she had so painstakingly built for herself and Oliver these past four years was in jeopardy.

It *was* in jeopardy! It had been in jeopardy since the moment Luca de Salvatore learnt that Oliver was his son!

She swallowed hard. 'Very well, Luc. I'll come to your vineyard with you tomorrow. But only on the understanding that...that there will be no repeat of...of this evening's behaviour.' Embarrassed colour burned Annie's cheeks just at the thought of the intimacies they had shared earlier.

He looked at her thoughtfully. 'Do you believe that to be possible?'

'It had better be, or I'm not coming to Venice with you!' Annie insisted stubbornly.

Luc studied her between narrowed lids as he once again noted the disarray of her hair, her lips swollen from the force of the kisses they had shared and the press of her breasts against that body-hugging white T-shirt, the nipples still hard and aroused.

This woman had caught fire in his arms in the lift this afternoon. And she'd continued to burn only a short time ago, when she had been so aroused by their lovemaking she had reached a climax that had shaken the whole of her body with its intensity.

Just as he had almost done as she'd kissed and caressed him…

Even during those wild years of his youth Luc could not remember being as aroused, so out of his own control, as he had been when Annie Balfour touched him with her hands and mouth.

Such loss of control had no place in the rigidly self-disciplined life of Luca de Salvatore!

He nodded. 'If that is your price for accompanying me to Venice, then I agree.'

She eyed him warily as she voiced her concern. 'A little too readily perhaps?'

He shrugged. 'I am acknowledging that, for the moment, physical intimacy between us only…confuses the issue, shall we say.'

Her cheeks coloured hotly. 'Might I remind you that *you're* the one who forced your way into *my* hotel suite this evening, Luc. You threatened both myself and my son—'

'*Our* son!'

'—before proceeding to make love to me in order to prove that *you still can*!' Annie continued fiercely, her eyes shooting sparks at him.

His jaw tightened. 'I did not—'

'Yes, you *did*, damn you!' She could never remember being this angry before. With anyone. 'Well, you've proved your point, Luc, and I've agreed to come to Venice with you tomorrow, now would you just *go*?'

Luc had no doubts that if he stayed they would just continue to argue. Or make love again. Neither of which was acceptable to him in his present mood.

Annie Balfour had managed to pierce his guard this evening. More than that, her caresses had driven him to the edge of a complete loss of control. He could not, would not, allow that to happen again.

He nodded coldly. 'I have your word that you will not leave the hotel and attempt to go back to England without me?'

Her eyes pierced him with their scorn. 'The Balfours have never run away from a fight either!'

'It is your intention to continue fighting me, then?'

'Oh, yes,' she stated confidently.

Luc shook his head. How could they possibly reach any sort of compromise, some agreement on the future, if they continued to argue and insult each other?

'Do you ever smile any more, Luc?' Annie eyed him curiously from behind her dark sunglasses.

She had been packed and ready to leave when Luc came to her suite shortly after ten o'clock, the grimness of his expression not in the least conducive to conversation. He had continued that grim silence as the convertible sports car he was driving ate up the miles to Venice, the beauty of the surrounding scenery obviously completely wasted on him.

And the longer that silence continued the more Annie became aware of him. Of how the darkness of his hair had become ruffled from the warmth of the breeze, giving him a boyish look so at odds with the coldness of his expression. Of the width of his shoulders beneath the black polo shirt he wore. The flatness of his abdomen. The long length of his muscled legs stretched out beside her own. The subtle male smell of him—an elusively tangy aftershave and raw masculinity—that was all Luc.

Damn it, Annie was just aware of everything about him!

'I smile when the occasion warrants it,' Luc answered her quietly.

'Really?' Annie jeered. 'Only I seem to remember you as being a lot more fun four years ago,' she added.

Black sunglasses hid the expression in Luc's eyes as he glanced at her. 'You gave me the impression yesterday evening that my conversation was not to your liking.'

'Not that conversation, no.' She grimaced. 'But a little polite conversation would be nice.'

'*Polite* conversation?' he repeated drily.

With the obvious implication that the two of them were incapable of being polite to each other.

Which they probably were, Annie acknowledged ruefully. Every conversation they now had seemed to come back to Oliver, and that was a subject on which they would never agree!

But not talking to each other at all certainly wasn't going to bring an end to that particular impasse.

'Yes, Luc, polite conversation,' she said. 'You comment on the warmth of the weather. I concur. You remark on the beauty of the countryside. I concur—'

'I do not believe you capable of *concurring* with me twice in the course of a single conversation,' Luc goaded back.

'No. Well. You're probably right about that.' She sighed. 'OK, then we'll just agree that the scenery is beautiful.'

'The scenery *is* beautiful,' Luc repeated mockingly.

'You know, coming from you, that almost counted as

a joke,' Annie remarked lightly as she settled back in the leather seat. Arguing with Luc hadn't succeeded in making her any less physically aware of him, but it was certainly a diversion from that awkward silence!

Luc eyed her guardedly. 'You seem less...antagonistic, this morning.'

Something he found extremely suspicious after the way they had parted last night, when Annie had given him the distinct impression that she intended fighting him to the bitter end.

She looked both confident and beautiful this morning in a pale cream knee-length sundress that showed off her tanned arms and legs, the red lights in her hair appearing deeper in the warmth of the sun and her face bare of make-up.

She raised an eyebrow. 'Never heard of trying to make the best of a bad situation?'

Oh, yes, Luc had heard of it—he just found it disconcerting after her assurances yesterday evening that she intended making his life a living hell. Of course, she had also said that would come after he had forced her to marry him.

'And making the best of this bad situation involves you being pleasant to me for a change?' he asked.

'Telling you that you're no fun any more is being pleasant.'

'It is an improvement on being called a bastard, yes,' Luc drawled.

Her cheeks coloured warmly. 'As I recall, you were behaving like one at the time.'

Luc's mouth tightened. 'You gave me no choice.'

'Oh, you had a choice, Luc,' she snapped. 'I think you just enjoy being like that!'

'Do I take it that our attempt at polite conversation is over now?' he taunted.

'Without a doubt!' Annie turned to look out of the window beside her.

She had lain awake for hours last night trying to find a solution to this problem. A solution that was acceptable to both of them, and not just to Luc.

She had known yesterday evening that returning to England without him was a non-starter; he would only follow her there, and in doing so no doubt create the scandal Annie was trying so hard to avoid.

The insults and accusations they'd hurled at each other during their arguments certainly wasn't helping the situation either.

That left only reason. Calm, logical reason.

Annie didn't want to marry Luca de Salvatore any more than he really wanted to marry her. Therefore there must be another, more acceptable, solution to this problem. One that could only be discussed in an atmosphere of calmness.

Which, as well as trying to dispel her total physical awareness of Luc, was what Annie had been trying to create a few minutes ago.

'I'm sorry.'

'What?' Annie frowned as she turned to look at Luc.

He sighed. 'I said, I'm sorry. For being the cause of yet another argument between us,' he expanded as she still looked puzzled.

'That's what I thought you meant…'

Luc's mouth twisted at her obvious surprise at his apology. 'You just did not believe it.'

'Well, it's a little unusual, you have to admit,' she pointed out.

It *was* unusual for Luc to apologise. For anything. Making him every bit as arrogant as Annie had often accused him of being?

Had he always been this way? Annie didn't seem to think so if her remark about him having been more fun four years ago was any indication.

Damn it, he hadn't just been fun four years ago, he'd been reckless and totally lacking in all responsibility!

But what was he now?

According to Annie he was unsmiling, not fun and totally lacking in a sense of humour.

The time spent restoring the de Salvatore business empire to its former glory had consumed Luc's every waking moment. Luca de Salvatore had found no time for smiles. Or fun. Let alone maintaining a sense of humour.

He had no time for them now either!

Just as he had no time whatsoever for the desire he felt for this woman that yesterday evening had threatened every barrier he'd placed about all of his softer emotions.

'Perhaps,' he answered curtly. 'But I would not take it as the setting of a precedent.'

'Oh, don't worry, I won't,' Annie assured him sarcastically. 'I'm well aware that one apology from Luca de Salvatore has to go a long way.'

Luc's mouth tightened. 'You do not have a very good opinion of me, do you?'

She shrugged bare shoulders. 'I don't know you.'

'And what little you do know you obviously do not like!'

'I suggest you ask me that again in a couple of days.'

Luc very much doubted that anything he did or said during the next two days was going to change Annie Balfour's opinion of him.

CHAPTER EIGHT

'ADMIRING the view?'

That was exactly what Annie had been doing as she stood out on the balcony of the guest bedroom one of the maids had shown her to a few minutes ago. And she felt reluctant to turn from admiring that view—miles and miles of heady sweet-smelling vineyards as far as the eye could see, with the waterways and graceful architecture of Venice glittering in the distance.

The de Salvatore villa itself was set on the hillside, a beautiful two-storey terracotta-coloured house, built in a hacienda style, and surrounded by terraced gardens filled with an array of heady perfumed flowers, and a huge swimming pool sparkling temptingly behind the villa itself.

It was all so beautiful—the villa itself, the surrounding hills covered in vines and the mystery of Venice as tempting as a jewel.

Only Annie's reason for being here stopped her from fully enjoying them!

She sighed wistfully before turning to face Luc as he stood in the doorway from the bedroom out onto the balcony. 'Is it all yours?'

'As far as the eye can see.' He nodded. 'Perhaps you would like to go for a ride after lunch?'

'On horseback, quad bikes or motorbikes?' she prompted interestedly, having seen the employees in the vineyards use all three as transport during the past few minutes as she watched them moving from one set of vines to another.

'Any or all of them.' Luc stepped fully out onto the balcony, and Annie saw that he had changed out of the black trousers and shirt he had worn for travelling, and into a pair of cream linen trousers and a brown short-sleeved shirt that emphasised the powerful width of his shoulders and muscled arms, and left his feet bare on the cool marble.

Dark sunglasses were pushed up into the dark thickness of hair still damp from the shower he had obviously taken before changing, allowing Annie an unimpeded view of those enigmatic dark eyes, and the harsh beauty of his face.

All in all, Luc looked good enough to eat!

Warm colour flared in Annie's cheeks as she remembered how close she had come to doing exactly that the evening before. 'I don't mind which,' she answered him abruptly, making no move to step away from the balustrade, knowing that if she did she might just forget her need to keep her physical distance from this man.

Something she hadn't succeeded in doing too well earlier in the confines of the car, their brief conversation having done very little to alleviate her discomfort. By the time they reached the villa Annie was so aware of her need to touch Luc that as soon as the maid left her alone in the bedroom she had rushed to the adjoining bathroom to splash cold water on her face in an effort to cool that fevered longing.

A need that had returned the moment Luc stepped out onto the balcony. In fact, the only thing holding Annie back from the ever-growing urge to go to him and curve her body intimately into his before taking his mouth was the painful thought that Oliver's future rested on what transpired between herself and Luc in the next few days.

Luc shrugged. 'Quad bikes or motorbikes, then. It will still be a little too warm for the horses immediately after lunch.'

'Fine.'

He frowned at her shortness. 'You seem... a little tense.'

Annie moistened suddenly dry lips. 'Do I?'

She wasn't tense—she was just painfully aware of Luc! Totally, achingly physically aware of him.

Luc studied her through narrowed lids. 'This bedroom is not to your liking?'

Having grown up either living or staying in one of the Balfour homes—several houses in London, the apartment in New York, a chalet at Klosters, even a privately owned Caribbean island—Annie was used to being surrounded by luxury.

Even so, the bedroom she had been given in the de Salvatore villa was something else—peach-coloured marble floors, beautiful white and gold antique furniture, including a four-poster bed draped in silk curtains. And the adjoining marble-floored bathroom was equally as magnificent, dominated as it was by a huge sunken bath surrounded by plants and statuary.

'What's not to like?' Annie replied honestly.

'Then perhaps you are just hungry for your lunch?' Luc persisted with concern.

'Maybe,' she said evasively, knowing ruefully that *he* was what she really hungered for. 'I need to call my mother and tell her where I am first though.'

'I should have thought earlier.' Luc looked annoyed with himself. 'There is a telephone downstairs in my study you may use for your call when you are ready.'

'Do I have time to freshen up and change before we eat?'

'But of course.' Luc nodded, sure that he was not imagining the return of Annie's caution around him. She almost seemed afraid of his proximity. 'As we parted some while ago I had thought you would have had time to have already done so.'

'I'm a woman, Luc,' she pointed out tartly. 'Worse than that, a Balfour woman! There are only three bathrooms at the chalet at Klosters,' she went on to explain as Luc raised a questioning brow. 'One of which my father, as the only male, claims for himself. When all the sisters are there together you should hear the fights over who gets to use the other two bathrooms first!'

Luc found himself smiling slightly at the image she presented. 'I wouldn't know—I'm an only child.'

Annie eyed him curiously. 'Isn't that unusual in an Italian family?'

He nodded. 'My mother was unable to have any more children after I was born.' His jaw tightened. 'A fact that probably contributed to my being a spoilt brat.'

'Were you a spoilt brat, Luc?' she asked gently.

'Like often recognises like, does it not?' Luc goaded.

Her eyes widened. 'If that was a dig at me, then you really don't know me at all either!'

He looked at her closely. 'Your clothes, even those business suits you wore over the weekend, have a designer label. Your hair is expertly—and no doubt expensively—styled. You go on family holidays to the family-owned chalet at Klosters and a private Caribbean island. You travel first class. Stay in exclusive suites in five-star hotels. You apparently know how to ride a horse, a quad bike and a motorbike, and no doubt many other things besides. I do not believe that the average young lady of twenty-four has the opportunity to do all, or perhaps any, of those things. So yes, I believe you are spoiled to a certain extent.'

Annie raised her chin challengingly. 'My father believes that in business the look is everything, hence the clothes, the hair and the first-class travel and five-star hotels. He also owns the chalet in Klosters, and the Caribbean island, not me. My stepfather taught me to ride a horse when I was six. My older sisters, the quad bike and motorbike when I was ten or so. Along with sailing and surfing, rock climbing and abseiling—'

'No wonder your father's hair has turned white!' Luc drawled.

'—but I believe those things make me accomplished rather than a spoilt brat,' Annie continued stubbornly. 'I also studied hard to get three straight As in my A levels. I went to university and attained my degree in English—'

'And became an unmarried mother three months later,' Luc finished for her.

'We've already had this conversation once, Luc,' she reminded him irritably.

Because Luc had not given any thought to contraception the night they spent together. Because he had left her so abruptly the following day. Because he had not bothered to try to find her again once his father was out of danger and recovering from his heart attack. Because he had been too focused on salvaging and then rebuilding the de Salvatore business empire to give more than a cursory thought to the girl called Annie that he had made love to that night…

His expression was bleak. 'I am doing everything I can to rectify that mistake—'

'You believe Oliver was a *mistake*?' Annie's voice was dangerously calm—the calm before the storm, in fact.

'I did not say that.'

'Oh, yes, you did!' Her eyes glittered deeply blue, and her hands were clenched at her sides.

'No—'

'Yes!' Annie bit out furiously, finding a temporary release from her tension—and her physical awareness of Luc—in her anger.

His face darkened ominously. 'You are becoming agitated…'

'We mothers tend to do that when someone attacks or criticises our child,' she pointed out.

A nerve pulsed in Luc's tightly clenched jaw as he looked at her coldly. 'I would never attack or criticise either my son or his mother.'

Not Oliver and Annie, but 'my son or his mother.'

Because Oliver as Luc's son was still an unknown quantity to him, and Annie was merely the vessel by which he had acquired that son.

The anger left her as quickly as it had arrived, leaving her feeling strangely weary. 'I really would like to take a shower and change my clothes now, Luc.'

It was impossible for him to miss the flatness of her tone. Or the sudden pallor of her cheeks. 'It was never my intention to hurt you, Annie—'

'Too late,' she choked.

Luc could see the tears glistening on her long dark lashes now. Annie's anger and sarcasm he could cope with; her tears were another matter entirely....

He took a step towards her. 'Annie—'

'Don't touch me, Luc,' she advised softly as she held up a hand to ward him off. 'I'm hanging on by a thread here,' she added shakily. 'The least show of kindness on your part could result in my blubbering all over you.'

Luc gave a pained frown. 'I believe my shoulders are strong enough to take it,' he assured her gruffly.

'I'm sure they are,' she replied. 'But my self-esteem isn't,' she added ruefully.

Luc looked at her wordlessly for several long seconds. He had been stunned yesterday when he learnt Annie had a son. Furiously angry once he had looked at those photographs of that dark-haired little boy, and realised from his date of birth that Oliver was his son too.

He was only now beginning to see, to realise, what that discovery on his part—his demand that she marry him—meant to Annie.

By insisting on marriage Luc would be taking her and Oliver away from everything and everyone that was familiar to them, at the same time forcing her into a role she obviously wanted no part of.

But what choice did Luc have except to demand she marry him? Oliver was indisputably his son, and the de Salvatore heir. Luc could not, would not, give Oliver up just because Anna Balfour managed to shed a few tears at the idea of becoming his wife!

'I will show you to my study so that you might telephone your mother when you come downstairs.'

Dark lashes fanned down on the paleness of her cheeks.

'Thank you,' she murmured huskily.

He looked momentarily confused. 'For allowing you to use the telephone?'

'No.' Annie looked up to give him a tremulous smile. 'For allowing me to keep my self-esteem.'

Luc drew in a ragged breath as he once again fought the urge to take Annie in his arms and offer her comfort. Knowing that if he held her in his arms it would not be comfort he offered her!

He wanted her. Wanted her with a fierceness that made the blood burn in his veins and his body ache. Wanted to make love to her, until both of them were too weak to do anything more but fall asleep in each other's arms.

It was a feeling so at odds with the man he had become these past four years—cold, ruthless, in control of all his emotions—that Luc knew he had to get out of here. Now. Before he could no longer resist giving in to that impulse he had to lay Annie down naked on the bed before caressing and kissing every inch of her.

His hands clenched into fists at his sides at the thought of gazing into the misty unfocused blue of Annie's eyes as she trembled and quaked in the throes of her climax. 'Please believe me when I say I am no longer that spoilt young man who let you down, Annie,' he said.

'Why aren't you?'

Luc's mouth thinned. 'It is a long story that does not reflect well on me.'

'But maybe one that you'll share with me someday?' she pressed gently.

'Perhaps.' He nodded. 'I will wait for you on the terrace.' Luc turned on his heel and left, knowing that if Annie were ever to understand the man he was now, the man he had become, then he would have to tell her of those dark days after his father's collapse. And then she'd know he was responsible for almost killing his own father....

'So which did you decide upon?' Annie asked lightly once they had finished eating the delicious cold lunch Luc's housekeeper had provided for them to enjoy on the terrace beside the sparkling blue pool.

She had kept her telephone call to Tilly deliberately brief, just telling her mother that she had met up with an old friend who had invited her to stay at their villa near Venice for a couple of days. As expected, Tilly had assured Annie she was more than happy to look after Oliver. With the added comment that a couple of days' holiday would do Annie the world of good.

Some holiday!

Annie had deliberately kept up a stream of inane chatter once she had joined Luc outside, more than a little embarrassed by the way she had almost broken down in front of him earlier. The reason for that emotional blip was obvious, of course—too much stress and too little sleep.

Along with that overwhelming attraction to Luc that was never far beneath the surface of her emotions.

Even now Annie was completely aware of everything about him. Of the way the darkness of his hair curled slightly from having dried in the warmth of the sun. How the hue of his olive skin had already deepened in the sunlight. Of the dark hair visible on his arms and at the V of his polo shirt. Of the way the thin material of that shirt emphasised the broadness of his shoulders and the washboard flatness of his abdomen.

As for his hands…

Annie found herself mesmerised by the lean strength of those long, tapered fingers as Luc ate, unable to stop herself from remembering how they'd felt on her body the evening before as he'd cupped her breasts before moving lower to caress her between her moist and aching thighs—

'Quad bike or motorbike?' she prompted again as her cheeks burned at the thought of what had happened next.

'You choose,' Luc invited as he sat back in his chair, the expression in his eyes once again hidden behind dark sunglasses.

'Quad bikes can be fun, but I'd enjoy using motorbikes, if that's OK with you?' She looked enquiringly at Luc.

'Fine,' Luc drawled. 'Although I have to admit, I haven't ridden one in years,' he added ruefully.

Annie quirked a pointed brow. 'Four and a half years to be precise?'

'As it happens…yes.'

'Hmm.' She frowned slightly. 'So what happened to change your lifestyle from that of irresponsible playboy to ruthless businessman?'

Luc scowled darkly at her perception. 'Like you, I grew up,' he brushed her off.

'But there must have been a reason for it?' she persisted. 'Didn't de Salvatore Enterprises hit a rough patch around that time?' she said slowly.

Luc eyes narrowed behind his sunglasses. 'How do you know that?'

She gave a shrug. 'I'm my father's daughter, remember? Besides, it isn't exactly a secret that you took over your father's ailing company and made it bigger and better than ever.'

'Not before *I* had almost ruined it!' Luc grated. 'At twenty-six I believed myself to be invincible,' he explained bluntly. 'I made many mistakes because of that belief. Mistakes that almost cost my father his life as well as his business empire.'

'What do you mean?' Annie gasped.

'Because of my mistakes my father had a heart attack and almost died,' Luc said bitterly. 'Does that not fit in with your image of me as the monster who is trying to take your son away from you?'

She looked at him directly. 'Oliver is your son too, Luc.'

'Yes,' he murmured. 'As I tried to tell you last night, I have no wish to hurt you, Annie. I just—I would like to be a father to Oliver. To help him to understand that although he has a privileged life, it does not mean he should behave as recklessly as I did for so many years.'

'You want to help him to not make the same mistakes that you did?'

'That is exactly what I want, yes,' he said. Luc had learned a hard lesson that he would never allow himself to forget.

Annie looked up at Luc quizzically, understanding the changes in him a little better now than she had. Understanding the compulsion he felt to be a full-time father to Oliver a little better than she had before too.

But still not enough to agree to marry him!

She gave a rueful sigh. 'I'm ready if you are?'

'You intend going out like that?' He looked at the white shorts and tank top, which was the same colour blue as her eyes, Annie had changed into after taking her shower.

Annie laughed. 'Is there something wrong with what I'm wearing?'

His mouth compressed. 'The employees at the vineyard would perhaps expect to see my future wife wearing something a little more…conservative, shall we say, than brief shorts and an even briefer top.'

'Really?' Annie said, unruffled. 'Well, as that future wife isn't going to be me, that expectation doesn't apply, does it?'

'It *does* apply to you—'

'No,' Annie cut in sharply. 'No, Luc, it doesn't,' she repeated firmly. 'Now are you ready to go out or not?' she asked again.

Luc looked down at her in frustration. There was no doubting that Annie looked fresh and cool in the brief shorts and tank top that emphasised the full curve of her breasts, slender waist and curvy hips, and the long length of her bare and golden-tanned legs.

She also looked no older than the twenty she had been the day Luc first met her.

And just as desirable!

The fact that her hair was secured on the crown of her head in an untidy tumble of chestnut curls, her face completely bare of make-up, the sun having brought out an endearing sprinkling of freckles on the bridge of her nose, should have had the opposite effect. Instead Luc ached to release those red-brown curls and let them cascade onto the bareness of her shoulders. Longed to kiss each and every one of those freckles before capturing her mouth hungrily with his and kissing her senseless.

Perhaps it had been a mistake to bring Annie here, to the de Salvatore villa in the hills above Venice. Luc had done so with the intention of them being able to talk, to discuss Oliver's future—and their own—without distractions.

He had not expected that same lack of distraction to have intensified his awareness of Annie, of her perfume and the smooth silkiness of her skin, skin he ached to touch to such a degree that Luc knew he had thought of little else but making love to her again since their arrival here.

He looked haughtily down the length of his nose at her. 'If it does not bother you to parade yourself around in public half naked, then I see no reason why it should bother me either.'

Annie's mouth tightened at what she knew to be a deliberate—and successful—attempt at an insult on Luc's part. 'Being seen half naked in public has never bothered a Balfour,' she retorted naughtily. 'In fact, being completely naked has never been too much of a problem for us either!'

Luc's nostrils flared disdainfully. 'Thank you for the timely reminder that you are a Balfour.'

'No problem.' She gave a breezy smile to hide how much it stung to hear the disgust in his voice. 'Although you might want to actually get to know some of those Balfours before you look down your disapproving nose at all of us.'

His mouth twisted. 'I know *you*, and that is enough.'

Annie drew in a sharp breath at this second deliberate and even more successful insult in as many minutes. 'What a pity, then, that your son is also a Balfour.'

Luc scowled. 'Not for too much longer.'

'You might be surprised!'

'I rarely am,' Luc drawled confidently.

Annie shook her head in disbelief. He really was the most arrogant, pig-headed, son of a— 'Then this could be a first,' she snapped.

Just when she thought she might actually be starting to like Luc, he reverted to type once again!

He had been much softer earlier as they had talked on the balcony of her bedroom, and then again just now as he spoke of his father, so much so that Annie had almost forgotten her reason for being here with him.

They were obviously lapses that Luc regretted, because he was back to being a bastard with a vengeance now!

CHAPTER NINE

'THAT was fun!' Annie laughed glowingly up at Luc a couple of hours later as they parked the motorbikes back in the storage shed several terraces down from the villa where the hay for the horses was also stored.

It had been fun to ride the motorbikes around the estate, Luc acknowledged with a slight frown. It had felt good to feel the wind in his hair and the warmth of the sun on his face. It had brought it home to Luc that fun really hadn't been a part of his life for a long time now.

Working twenty hours a day, enjoying the occasional woman in his bed, followed by yet more work, had been what was necessary to return the de Salvatore business empire back to the thriving concern it had once been.

That it now was.

Yet Luc still more often than not worked those twenty-hour days. Because, apart from his ageing parents, he'd had nothing else in his life?

Something that no longer applied now that he knew he had a son.

Just as he was determined that Annie Balfour would soon become his wife. His to kiss and to touch whenever he wanted...

Having decided yesterday that such distractions only confused the situation, Luc had almost been driven mad with a desire to do both those things this afternoon as he watched Annie from behind the shield of his sunglasses. The way the bareness of her thighs had hugged either side of the leather seat of the motorbike. The creamy swell of firm, unconfined breasts visible above the low neckline of her top…

'Luc?' Annie prompted lightly at his continued silence.

He grimaced as he turned to face her, having pushed his sunglasses up into the dark thickness of his hair so that he could see in the gloom of the shed. 'Sorry, I was thinking of something else.'

Well, of course he was, Annie acknowledged ruefully. No doubt wishing himself far away from here. And the inconvenience of having to entertain her.

She shrugged. 'I could go for a swim now if there's something else you would rather do?'

The intensity of his gaze swept over her, slowly, lingering on the curve of her breasts. 'What did you have in mind?' he asked huskily.

Annie found herself slightly unnerved by the heat in Luc's eyes. Deep, fathomless dark eyes that she might drown in if she continued to look at him.

So she shifted her own gaze to a point over his left shoulder. 'I thought maybe—' She moistened suddenly dry lips. 'I'm sure the vineyard doesn't run itself.'

'No, I have a manager who does that,' Luc drawled.

'Oh.' Annie was suddenly very aware of how alone they were in the cool gloom of the shed, and the delicious shiver that ran down the length of her spine was due to the heat of Luc's gaze rather than that coolness.

He frowned. 'You are cold—'

'No, of course I'm not cold!' Annie winced at the awkwardness of her reply. 'I…well…maybe a little.'

It was just so eerily quiet in here—quiet and private. Annie doubted that anyone ever had reason to come down here at this time of day. 'We should probably go back up to the villa now.'

'Should we?'

Annie shot Luc a cautious glance. When had he moved so that he now stood so close she had to tilt her head back to look up at his face? More to the point, *why* had he moved?

She moistened her lips nervously as she took another step back. 'I really think we should get back now, Luc—'

'There is no reason to rush.' His accented English had become more apparent as his voice lowered seductively. 'I do not like your hair confined like this,' he murmured softly even as his hand reached up and removed the clasp from the crown of her head.

Annie was aware both of her hair tumbling loosely onto her shoulders and the way Luc's eyes had become darker still as he entwined his fingers in the hair at her nape and began to pull her slowly towards him.

'I— What are you doing, Luc?' she gasped.

He gave a wolfish smile. 'Guess,' he whispered, so close now that the warmth of his breath brushed against her lips.

'I thought we had agreed that…that this only confused the issue.' Annie could hear the desperation in her own voice as she tried to resist him.

'This…?' Once again his breath was a warm caress,

against Annie's jaw this time as he bent his head to place feather-light kisses along its length.

Annie raised protesting hands against Luc's chest with the intention of pushing him away, those hands stilling instead, lingering to caress, as she felt the hardness of muscle encased in silk, his heart a wild and primitive beat beneath her fingertips. 'You agreed we weren't going to do this again.'

'I have changed my mind,' he murmured as his hands moved to cup her bottom and pull her into him, making her completely aware of the hard, urgent throb of his arousal.

An arousal echoed in the sudden explosion of heat between Annie's own thighs. 'But—'

'Can you not see that this is the only way in which we seem able to communicate?' He groaned even as his mouth took possession of hers, fiercely, hungrily.

Annie's hands crushed against Luc's chest as her lips parted to meet the full force of that kiss. A kiss that became more urgent still as his arousal hardened further until all Annie could think about was having him deep inside her.

She parted her legs as Luc pressed closer still in an attempt to fill her emptiness, the velvet hardness of his shaft a hard and rhythmic caress against the tiny nub nestled there.

This was madness. Pure madness. But it was a madness that Annie had no will, or desire, to resist.

Instead her hands moved up so that she could entangle her fingers in the dark thickness of Luc's hair as he drew her bottom lip into his mouth, gently biting and then sucking that tender flesh. His hands moved up to slip the thin straps of her top down her arms before pushing the material down to her waist and baring her breasts.

Annie gasped slightly as the cool air caressed her heated flesh, the sensitive nipples already aroused, becoming even more so as Luc cupped those twin orbs, and the soft pad of his thumb swept lightly, teasingly, across those tender tips. Again. And again. Until Annie was lost in that mindless need.

She pressed herself against his skilful hands. 'Please, Luc,' she moaned.

'Tell me what you want,' Luc encouraged hoarsely. 'Tell me, Annie!'

'Harder,' she pleaded encouragingly. 'Harder, Luc!' She arched her back, her breasts thrusting once again against his hands.

Luc's eyes glittered darkly as he looked down at her breasts, the areolae surrounding the nipples a deep dusky pink, those nipples dark and swollen, like two ripe berries waiting to be tasted. Eaten.

His head lowered so that he might taste one of those berries, taking it fully into his mouth while his hand rolled its twin between thumb and finger. Annie groaned deeply and rubbed her thighs urgently against the rock hardness of Luc's.

Luc transferred the attention of his lips, tongue and teeth to Annie's other nipple before moving his hand down to the fastening of her shorts and sliding the zip down over silky panties to cup and caress the moist heat between her thighs.

'Yes! Oh, yes, Luc!' she encouraged breathlessly as she pushed those clothes down the length of her smooth legs before stepping out of them completely.

Her curls were silky soft to the touch as Luc sought,

and found, the swollen bud nestled there, feeling it pulse beneath his fingers as he stroked her. He could hear the ragged sob in Annie's breathing, her fingers tightening as she clung to his shoulders, and she arched into him in rhythm with those caresses.

Annie cried out as Luc slid first one finger, and then two, into her hot wetness, plunging into her again and again as the soft pad of his thumb stroked against her aching bud. He continued to tease her nipple with his teeth and tongue, taking Annie higher and higher until she knew herself poised on the edge of release.

'Come for me, *cara*,' Luc encouraged urgently as he raised his head from her breast. 'Let me watch you as you come!'

His eyes glittered in triumph as she cried out suddenly, climaxing fiercely, endlessly, until she collapsed weakly against his chest.

She clung to Luc's shoulders as he lifted her, wrapping her legs about his waist as his hands cupped her bare bottom and he carried her across to where some bails of hay were stored in one corner of the shed. His gaze held hers as he slowly lowered her to the floor and then ripped the shirt from his body and placed it on the hay. Then he carefully laid her down on his shirt before straightening to take off the rest of his clothes.

Annie's breath caught in her throat when he finally stood naked above her. There was a silky covering of dark hair on his chest, the muscles deeply defined, his hips lean, the long length of his shaft jutting out in a hard, throbbing arousal that Annie longed to touch.

She moved up onto her knees in front of him, her gaze holding his as she reached out to cup him, her other hand caressing his silken length, and then running her thumb softly across its sensitive tip.

Luc groaned low in his throat as the muscles in his buttocks and thighs tensed and his back and neck arched. 'No!' His hands moved to cup either side of Annie's face to hold her away from him as she would have taken him in her mouth. 'I want to be inside you. I *need* to be inside you…' he growled as he moved down onto the straw to stretch out and pull Annie on top of him so that several inches of him slid into her hot tightness. 'Take me, Annie,' he encouraged. 'All of me…'

She looked magnificent as she raised herself slightly so that her hand could guide him deeper inside her, her hair a red-brown tangle about her shoulders, eyes sultry, lips swollen, and her breasts pouting temptingly.

Luc gave another strangled groan, and his eyes closed in pleasure as he slid inside her and he felt her wrap around him, taking him in until she sheathed him fully.

Luc took a few moments to just enjoy the sensation of being inside her. She was so hot. So wet. So incredibly, wonderfully tight.

And then she began to move. Lifting herself up to slide along the length of his shaft until the tip was poised at her entrance, before plunging down to once again take him fully inside her. Holding his gaze with hers, she repeated the movement, riding him slowly at first, and then faster, harder, her breasts moving in the same mesmerising rhythm.

Luc raised his head to kiss one breast as Annie continued to move over him. His hands clasped her hips as his thighs surged up to meet each downward stroke until he felt an unmistakable inner tremor.

That tremor became a full-blown quake as Annie's climax claimed her, stronger, longer, than the last one, and Luc cried out as she finally took him over that precipice with her.

Only the ragged sounds of their breathing broke the silence as Annie lay replete and exhausted on Luc's chest, his skin warm and slightly damp beneath her cheek as his chest quickly rose and fell.

Dear God, after all they had said—all the insults—it had happened again!

Only this time it had been worse—or did she mean better?

Surely making love couldn't get much better than this? It couldn't possibly; if it had been any more enjoyable, if Annie had felt any more pleasure, climaxed any more intensely than she had, then she surely would have expired completely!

Yes, but what happened now? What did Luc think was going to happen after…after— Oh, dear Lord, she had all but begged him to take her, had let him gaze at her unashamedly as she'd writhed in ecstasy above him.

'What?' Luc looked up dazedly as Annie sat up, his hair falling endearingly over his forehead, dark eyes as warm as melted chocolate, and the hard sensuality of his lips relaxed into a half-smile.

It was all Annie could do to stop herself from bending down and capturing those lips again with her own. 'We need to get dressed, Luc,' she told him instead. 'Anyone might come in here and find us together like this.'

'Not at this time of day,' Luc reassured her huskily, his hands on her hips as he rolled slightly to the side, taking Annie with him so that she now lay beside him, one of her legs still hooked about his hips, their bodies touching from their chests to their joined thighs. 'Love-making should be savoured. Enjoyed...'

'I think we've savoured and enjoyed enough for one day,' she said sharply as she attempted to extricate her body from his. 'Let me go, Luc,' she ordered as he only tightened his arms to keep her in place.

He frowned as he finally saw the fierce glitter of her eyes and the angry flush in her cheeks. 'And if I refuse?'

'Why would you?' she asked sarcastically. 'You've had me now, so there's no reason for us to stay here any longer!'

'*Had* you?' he uttered incredulously.

Annie pursed her lips. 'Had sex with me, then, if you prefer.'

His eyes narrowed. 'And what if I wish to have sex with you again?'

She snorted. 'I'm sure that wasn't part of the plan.'

He drew in a sharp, hissing breath. 'You think, as all my other arguments have failed, that it was my plan to *seduce* you into submission?'

'Wasn't it?' she challenged accusingly.

Luc hadn't been able to plan *anything*, it seemed, since meeting Annie Balfour again! Even his work, his driving force, no longer held the same appeal when he knew she was somewhere near.

He certainly hadn't planned to make love with her this afternoon; he just didn't seem to be able to stop himself from touching her, taking her, whenever the opportunity arose.

So much for his decision not to do any of those things

again until they had settled the question of marriage between them!

He reached out to clasp Annie's arms so that he might lift her up and away from him, his jaw tightening as his body protested at being removed from the hot tightness of hers. He stood abruptly to pull on body-hugging boxers before speaking again. 'I believe I might equally accuse you of endeavouring to seduce me into doing as *you* wish!'

'Attempting to make you my sex slave, you mean?' she retorted with obvious derision.

Luc made a dismissive movement of his shoulders. 'I am sure that many men would agree to anything you asked of them if you rewarded them as generously as you have just rewarded me.' His dark gaze swept lingeringly over her nakedness.

Annie drew in a sharp breath even as she stared up at him in disbelief. Luc couldn't really think that; for heaven's sake, she didn't have enough experience with men to even contemplate attempting such a calculated plan!

'Doesn't that usually work better if the woman asks for what she wants *before* they make love?'

'Usually.' His mouth quirked. 'But then our relationship has been…unusual, from the first.'

Annie felt the heat burn her cheeks at the memory of just how unusual it had been. That wild, impetuous night four and a half years ago. Their unexpected, tempestuous meeting again at Lake Garda. Luc's demand, once he learnt of Oliver's existence, that she become his wife…

Wasn't all of that complication enough without her

succumbing to his arrogant brand of seduction every time he so much as touched her?

She sighed heavily as she stood to begin pulling on her own clothes. 'The only thing I want from you, Luc, is for you to leave Oliver and me to live our lives in peace, and I already know that isn't going to happen.'

He gave a smug smile. 'Not this side of the next millennium, no.'

Annie gave him a frustrated glare as she finished pulling on her top before once again looking on the floor for the clasp that had held her hair in place at her crown. 'I would like to go back to the villa now,' she said stiffly.

'Of course,' he accepted, just as distantly.

How had this happened? Annie wondered as she hurriedly preceded Luc up the steps to the villa. One minute they were as close as two human beings could possibly be, and the next they couldn't be far enough apart. Emotionally as well as physically.

Physically!

She blushed just at the memory of the intimacies they had so recently shared. Squirmed inside because her body still tingled and ached from the force of their lovemaking. Was this how it was going to be between them? Mind-blowing hot sex followed by a return of the fraught tension that told Annie, at least, that they were actually worlds apart?

The sooner Luc accepted that Annie wasn't going to marry him, the better it would be for both of them!

And what happened once he *had* accepted that? Would he then go ahead with his threat of a legal battle over Oliver? One glance back at the brooding coldness of Luc's expression told her that he would do exactly that.

No doubt once again making a huge Balfour family scandal appear in the front-page headlines of all the newspapers.

Her father was just going to *love* that! He—

'Signor de Salvatore!' The elderly housekeeper hurried from the back of the house the moment Annie and Luc stepped inside the villa's coolness, her face and hands animated as she continued talking to her employer.

Annie had studied Spanish, German and French when she was at school, her Italian only very rudimentary, but her attention was caught and held as she heard her own name in the older woman's conversation, followed seconds later by 'Signora Tilly Williams.'

'Luc...?' Annie prompted anxiously.

'*Grazie*, Maria.' He briskly dismissed the housekeeper before answering Annie. 'Your mother rang while we were...out.' His mouth firmed. 'She asks that you call her back on her mobile as soon as you return.'

Annie felt her face go pale at the knowledge she had only talked to her mother a few hours ago, that something must have happened to necessitate Tilly needing to speak to her again so soon.

CHAPTER TEN

LUC paced the drawing room restlessly as he waited for Annie to come back from his study after returning her mother's telephone call.

He had advised Annie not to jump to any conclusions, to just stay calm until she had spoken to her mother, but inwardly Luc was just as concerned by Tilly's call as Annie so obviously was.

From the little Annie had told him of her mother, Tilly Williams appeared to be a practical as well as warm woman; the fact that she had married Oscar Balfour knowing it was a marriage of convenience spoke of her practicality, and that she had done so out of love for his three young motherless daughters was testament to her warmth of nature.

As such, Luc couldn't imagine she would have telephoned Annie so quickly, when the two of them had only spoken a few hours ago, over some triviality.

One look at the pain and stress on Annie's face when she entered the drawing room was enough to tell Luc that his surmise was a correct one. 'What is it?' he barked.

'I have to leave, Luc,' she said. 'I need to get back to England as soon as possible.'

'We will both go to England once you have told me what has happened,' Luc insisted.

She shook her head. 'I don't have time for another argument, Luc.'

'There will be no argument if you just tell me what has happened!' he demanded forcefully as he crossed the room to grasp her firmly by the shoulders. 'Annie!' he said, his own fear growing by the second as he saw the tears now balanced on her long, dark lashes.

Annie seemed to focus on him with effort. 'I—' She moistened dry lips. 'Oliver accompanied Tilly to a gymkhana this afternoon. She only took her eyes off him for a second and—' She broke off, pressing a trembling hand to the back of her mouth.

'Tell me what has happened to Oliver!' Luc begged, almost beside himself with fear by now.

Annie swallowed hard, and made an effort to pull herself together, still desperately trying to take in Tilly's conversation herself. 'He was kicked by one of the horses and—' Luc released her so suddenly that she swayed a little. 'What are you doing?' she asked as Luc took out his mobile phone and began making a call.

'Readying the de Salvatore plane for immediate take-off, of course,' he said, turning away as his call was answered, to begin issuing a spate of instructions in Italian.

Annie was too worried and too full of self-recriminations to take too much notice of Luc's telephone conversation.

The tears fell hotly down her cheeks as she realised that all the time she and Luc had been making love, their son was injured and being rushed to hospital!

Annie would never forgive herself if anything

happened to Oliver. She should never have allowed her father to bully her into coming to Italy in the first place. She certainly shouldn't have let Luc force her into remaining on in Italy. If she had gone home this morning, then she would have accompanied Tilly and Oliver to the gymkhana and probably none of this would have happened.

As it was, Oliver—small, sturdy, vulnerable Oliver—was now unconscious in hospital with a possible concussion and who knew what else wrong.

'It will be all right, Annie.' Luc reached out to grasp both her hands firmly in his.

Annie's eyes flashed angrily as she pulled her hands away to glare across the table that separated them in the luxurious cabin of the de Salvatore jet. 'I realise you like to think of yourself as omnipotent, Luc, but you can't possibly know that!' she exclaimed, still too shaken by Tilly's news to be able to think of anything else—least of all the pallor of Luc's face that was clear evidence of his own concerns over Oliver.

'No, I don't,' Luc acknowledged as he sat back heavily in his seat. 'But your mother's second telephone call was much more reassuring.'

Tilly had managed to call them again before the plane took off to tell them that Oliver had woken up, sore and a little bewildered by his surroundings, but that the doctors now seemed pretty confident that there was going to be no lasting damage.

None of which reassured Annie in the slightest when she just wanted to hold her small son in her arms and know for herself that he really was going to be OK.

'Keep telling yourself that, Luc,' she said shakily,

still too angry and upset to be able to offer him the same comfort he was attempting to give her.

Luc knew that he well deserved the anger she was directing at him. She had not wanted to travel to Venice with him. *He* had been the one responsible for preventing her from returning home as she had wished.

Preventing her?

No, not just that; he had *insisted* that Annie stay on in Italy with him. Had assured her that he wouldn't allow her to return to England until she agreed to marry him. And now his son, that beautiful and dark-haired little boy that Luc had so far only seen in photographs, was in hospital after receiving a severe blow to the head.

Without the love and comfort he no doubt needed from his mother.

No wonder Annie continued to refuse to even consider his proposal; the ruthless arrogance Luc had shown her since they'd met each other again was even less acceptable than the reckless self-confidence he had so catastrophically demonstrated four and a half years ago!

If Oliver recovered—

When Oliver recovered, Luc firmly corrected himself. Then—

'I'm sorry, Luc.'

He was frowning darkly as he looked across the table and met Annie's contrite blue gaze. 'What can you possibly have to be sorry about?' he rasped.

Annie grimaced. Luc's few minutes of brooding silence had given her time enough to calm down and realise that she had been transferring her own worry and guilt over Oliver onto Luc.

When in reality *she* was the one who hadn't followed

through on her decision to leave Italy sooner. Admittedly in the belief that it would be easier to reason with Luc here rather than back at Balfour Manor. Nevertheless, she'd had a choice—and events had proved that she had obviously made the wrong one!

She bit her lower lip before admitting, 'Taking out my frustration with this situation on you isn't going to change anything.'

Luc's mouth thinned. 'Who else should you blame but me?'

Annie shook her head. 'I don't—' She broke off as the Italian captain of the plane began to speak. 'Please tell me that was an announcement that we're about to land?' She looked across at Luc anxiously.

He smiled. 'That was indeed an announcement that we are about to land,' he said.

'Thank God!' Annie breathed her relief.

The landing, passing through customs, the drive in the private car Luc had waiting for them and arriving at the hospital where Oliver had been admitted earlier today all passed in a blur as far as Annie was concerned.

She was barely aware of Luc holding her hand firmly in his as he strode along beside her. She hurried down the long corridor to the ward where her mother had told her Oliver had been admitted, Annie's only desire now to get to her son as soon as possible so that she could see for herself that he truly was going to be OK. Something she wouldn't feel sure about until she had actually held Oliver in her arms, despite having received another reassuring telephone call from Tilly just a few minutes ago.

Her mother, a slim and beautiful redhead in her late forties, stood in the corridor waiting for them, her face lighting up as soon as she saw Annie. 'He's going to be fine, darling,' Tilly soothed, as with a pained sob Annie rushed into her waiting arms.

Annie held on tightly to her mother as she finally allowed the tears of tension to fall hotly down her cheeks. 'Is he awake? Is he in pain? Can I—'

'You have to calm down before you go in to see him, Annie.' Her mother ran a soothing hand up and down her back. 'And yes, he's awake and asking for you. Just be prepared for the fact that he has a dressing over the stitches, and he's slightly woozy from the painkillers the doctor gave him.'

'I have to see him.' Annie pulled abruptly from her mother's arms, not sparing Luc so much as a second glance as she hurried into the room beyond where her beloved Oliver lay.

Leaving Luc to the curious gaze of the beautiful and petite woman, who with her long red hair and blue eyes was easily recognisable as Annie's mother.

Her mouth curved into a rueful smile. 'I apologise—my daughter usually has better manners.'

Luc inclined his head in acknowledgement. 'These are difficult circumstances.'

'Yes.' She gave a wistful sigh.

'I am Luca de Salvatore.' He politely offered his hand.

'Tilly Williams.' She returned the gesture, her hand cool and elegant in his. 'I've often seen your name mentioned in the business papers. You're the friend Annie was staying with in Italy?' It was impossible to miss the curiosity that sharpened her huskily low tone. Or the slight puzzlement in that intelligent blue gaze as she looked at him more closely.

No doubt wondering why it was that Luc seemed vaguely familiar to her. No doubt she would place that familiarity eventually!

Luc drew in a ragged breath, longing to go in and see Oliver for himself, but at the same time aware that the little boy didn't know him, and would no doubt be upset by the arrival of a stranger in his hospital room.

'Yes,' he confirmed simply.

'Strange that Annie has never mentioned you before,' Tilly said slowly, frowning a little now.

Luc settled for giving what he hoped was a noncommittal shrug.

'Have the two of you been friends for very long?' she pressed.

'We met some years ago, yes,' he answered evasively.

'I see,' Tilly murmured.

Luc's mouth twisted ruefully. 'Do you?'

'I believe so, yes.' She paused. Then she said, 'Would you like to go in and see Oliver, Mr de Salvatore?'

The suggestion confirmed that Tilly had realised exactly who Luc was. As she must also realise that he hadn't been a part of either Annie's or Oliver's lives for the past four and a half years.

He swallowed the lump that had suddenly appeared in his throat. 'I do not think Annie would appreciate my doing that.'

'Oh, I think that you'll find my daughter is big enough to accept that these are…unusual circumstances,' Tilly assured him drily. 'After all, she brought you here, didn't she?'

Luc grimaced. 'Once I learnt of Oliver's accident I gave her little choice in the matter, I am afraid.'

'Oh, you have no need to be afraid of me, Mr de Salvatore,' Tilly said lightly. 'My ex-husband is another matter, however! Or maybe not…' she added with slow deliberation.

'Sorry?'

'How did you and my daughter meet, Mr de Salvatore?' she questioned shrewdly.

'Recently? Or…before?' he asked awkwardly.

'Recently,' she clarified.

Luc was unaccustomed to explaining himself to anyone, but in these 'unusual circumstances' he accepted that perhaps he needed to. 'We attended the same business conference at Lake Garda.'

'Ah.' Tilly gave a knowing nod.

'I am sorry, but I do not—'

'Luc?'

He turned swiftly to see Annie standing in the doorway of the hospital room, her face still unusually pale but the tears no longer falling. Luc couldn't resist looking past her into the room beyond, where he could see the outline of a small boy lying in the bed, his curls dark against the white bandage about his temple.

Oliver.

His son.

Annie couldn't miss the way Luc's gaze moved so quickly past her to where Oliver lay, her heart aching at the hunger she saw in those dark eyes. 'Would you like to come in?' she invited gently.

That hungry black gaze moved back to her sharply. 'I would not like to cause Oliver any further distress by presenting him with a stranger.'

'He fell asleep once I had assured him that I would still be here when he woke up,' Annie explained.

A nerve pulsed in Luc's clenched jaw. 'In that case, I would very much like to see him.'

Annie nodded before glancing across at Tilly. 'Luc and I will sit with Oliver for a while, Mummy, if you would like to take a break?'

Tilly nodded. 'The battery on my mobile has gone flat, so I need to go home and call your father.'

Annie frowned. 'He isn't at Balfour Manor?'

'Is he ever nowadays?' Tilly said lightly.

Tilly was right; having dispatched his daughters to the four corners of the earth, Oscar now displayed a distinct reluctance to spend any time alone at Balfour Manor.

'I'll see you later, then, Mummy,' Annie said warmly.

'No doubt I'll see you both later, hmm?' Her mother gave Luc a pointed glance.

Annie groaned inwardly. People generally tended to underestimate Tilly because of her warmth and openness, but having helped her mother set up her small cookery business, Annie knew just how shrewd Tilly could be when it was necessary. No doubt her mother had taken one look at Luc, seen his resemblance to Oliver and guessed exactly who he was!

'No doubt,' she acknowledged drily. 'Luc?' She opened the door wider for him to enter, remaining by the closed door as Luc moved past her to cross silently to the bedside.

How must it feel for him to be looking down at his son for the first time? She found it difficult to imagine.

Luc couldn't breathe, and his heart seemed to have stopped beating altogether, as he looked down at the tiny child lying in a hospital bed that was far too big for him.

There was a bandage wrapped about Oliver's head,

of course, but what little Luc could see of the little boy's
dark curls reminded him of his own at the same age.
Delicate lids were closed over eyes Luc knew were as
deep a blue as his mother's, and long dark lashes rested
against chubby cheeks. Oliver's face still bore the rosy
plumpness of babyhood, a tiny little nose, a small bow of
a mouth and a little pointed chin. He was wearing colour-
ful pyjamas decorated with ponies, his hands spread like
starfish on top of the bedclothes.

His son.

His beautiful flesh-and-blood son!

Having given Luc a few moments' privacy Annie
now crossed the room to stand at his side to look down
at Oliver. She still trembled slightly with the relief of
having held her son in her arms, of seeing for herself
that he wasn't too distressed. In fact, apart from the
gash on his head that had needed several stitches, Oliver
didn't seem to have suffered any ill effects from his
accident.

'He's so small,' Luc murmured gruffly at her side.

'I shouldn't let him hear you say that,' Annie warned
drily as she moved to sit down on one of the chairs beside
the bed before taking one of Oliver's hands in her own,
needing that physical contact with him even though he
was asleep. 'Oliver considers himself quite the man of
the family at the gatehouse, and takes great delight in
ordering his grandmother and me around,' she explained
ruefully at Luc's questioning look. 'He's obviously inherited his father's ability to issue orders and expect them
to be obeyed!'

Luc moved to sit down on the chair on the other side
of the bed, his gaze still firmly fixed on Oliver as he
lay between them, fast asleep and breathing softly. 'Tell

me about him,' he invited hoarsely. 'How much did he weigh at birth? Was he a good baby? When did he get his first tooth? Take his first step?'

There was so much that Luc didn't know about Oliver, so much he had missed because she had decided not to try to find him all those years ago and tell him of Oliver's existence, Annie realised with a heavy feeling of guilt.

She did her best to correct that omission over the next half an hour or so as Oliver continued to sleep, the two of them interrupted at intervals by one of the nurses coming in to check on Oliver, as Annie related everything she could remember about the first three years and eight months of his life.

'He goes to the local playgroup in the village hall?' Luc raised dark brows as Annie related this piece of information.

She stiffened defensively. 'I already told you, I want Oliver to have as normal a life as possible.'

'Which includes going to playgroup with the local children of the village three mornings a week?'

She frowned. 'Yes.'

'The village of Balfour?'

'Your point being…?' She eyed him guardedly.

'Doesn't the fact that Oliver's surname is the same as the village rather detract from him just being another of the local children?' Luc asked softly.

Annie frowned her irritation. 'If you're trying to pick another argument, Luc—'

'I'm not,' he reassured her quickly. 'Having grown up as the de Salvatore heir, with a nanny and then numerous private tutors, I totally approve of your attempts to give Oliver a childhood free of such constraints.' He reached out and gently stroked one of the starfish little hands resting on the bed sheet, Oliver's skin feeling so soft and new that Luc felt the emotion rise at the back of his throat.

'Oh.'

Luc smiled as Annie once again had that look of a slightly deflated balloon. 'You did not expect that to be my response, did you?'

'In a word? No!' she said wryly.

'Your mother is…not as I had imagined her to be,' he said quietly, still gently stroking Oliver's hand.

'No,' Annie agreed. 'But don't be fooled by that maternal exterior. I assure you, she is much more astute than people give her credit for.'

Luc looked across at her searchingly. 'You realise that she has guessed who I am?'

'Oh, yes.' Tilly had made that perfectly obvious by that pointed glance she had given Annie earlier. 'I shouldn't worry too much about that though,' Annie added. 'It's hardly going to remain a secret for very long once you decide to make a legal claim on Oliver.'

He drew dark brows together. 'Does that mean you have definitely decided not to accept my marriage proposal?'

Annie drew in a sharp breath. 'You didn't make a marriage proposal, Luc.'

'Of course I—'

'No, Luc, you didn't,' she cut in firmly. 'You issued another one of those orders you're so fond of making: *You will be my wife and Oliver will be my son.* In typical Me Tarzan You Jane fashion!'

Luc scowled fiercely. 'Me Tarzan You Jane?'

Annie smiled wryly at the disbelief she could hear in his tone. 'I don't think here and now is the right time for us to talk about this.' She gave the still-sleeping Oliver a pointed glance.

'Me Tarzan You Jane...' Luc repeated again in disgust. 'Is that really how you think of me?'

How else was she supposed to think of him after the way he had behaved so dictatorially both at Lake Garda and then at his vineyards near Venice?

Not that he'd behaved like that all the time...

Annie felt the colour warm her cheeks as she thought of their lovemaking earlier today. So much had happened since then that it seemed like a lifetime ago!

It was a lifetime ago. A time out of time.

A time never to be repeated!

'Have you given me any reason since we met again not to think of you in that way?' she asked bluntly.

'This afternoon—'

'Was a mistake,' Annie interrupted quickly, her cheeks actually burning now. 'An enjoyable mistake at the time admittedly, but nevertheless still a mistake,' she insisted as Luc would have interrupted.

'I disagree.'

'Luc, can't you see that a physical relationship between us only clouds the issue?'

'That issue being...?'

'That we don't love each other!' Annie was breathing hard in her agitation.

Luc's eyes glittered darkly. 'Love may come with time.'

'Love either is or it isn't, Luc,' Annie said. 'And in our case, it isn't,' she added wearily.

Or, to be more precise, in Luc's case it wasn't.

Annie had had plenty of time to think during that long journey back to England. And not all of it had been about her worry over Oliver. Mainly because to think of Oliver was to now think of Luc too, the two of them inexplicably bound together in her mind.

Luc and Oliver.

Oliver and Luc.

And she had realised during that tense flight back to England that she loved them both.

Not in the same way, of course.

As Oliver's mother she loved him unconditionally. But these past two days, this afternoon especially when Luc had talked to her about his father, of his reasons for wanting to be Oliver's father, when Annie had become completely unravelled in Luc's arms, she had also come to realise that she had fallen in love with him, despite the arrogance and coldness that now seemed such an integral part of his nature.

CHAPTER ELEVEN

'YOUR mother is a warm and understanding woman,' Luc remarked admiringly as he and Annie made up the two beds that had been provided so that they could remain at the hospital overnight with Oliver.

Her mother was a warm and *manipulative* woman, Annie inwardly corrected. She would much rather Tilly had put Luc up for the night at either the gatehouse or Balfour Manor, but her mother had suggested that, in the circumstances, perhaps Luc might prefer to remain at the hospital overnight too.

In the circumstances...

Even though the subject hadn't been openly discussed between the three adults when Tilly returned to the hospital earlier, they all knew what those circumstances were!

Luc was Oliver's father, so of course he would want to stay here overnight.

Although the good news was that so far Oliver had shown no evidence of the concussion the doctors had feared, and if that continued to be the case, then they intended to discharge him the following morning.

But not before Annie had spent the night at the hospital with Luc.

Admittedly they would be sleeping in separate beds, and Oliver's presence was more than enough to ensure there would be no repeat of this afternoon's madness. But Annie's newly realised feelings for Luc made her self-consciously aware of how alone they were in the quiet of this private hospital room. Of how much she loved him...

Had she always loved him?

Four and a half years ago Annie had been completely bowled off her feet by the rakish and exciting Luc. Had realised once she returned home from her ski trip that one glance had been all it had taken for her to fall in love with him. For her to have behaved completely out of character by spending the night with him.

But had she continued to be in love with Luc for all this time?

Her lack of interest in going out with other men, and her disappointment in the few she had dated, all seemed to indicate that she had.

Annie now glanced across at Luc beneath lowered lashes as he placed his overnight bag on top of the bed before unzipping it to look through its contents.

No. She glanced across at Luca de Salvatore.

Because this man, so darkly brooding, so much in control of both himself and his surroundings, was not the devil-may-care Luc that Annie had met and fallen in love with.

So did that mean that in the past two days she had fallen in love with Luca de Salvatore too?

God, it was all so complicated. So confusing. Luca de Salvatore and Luc were one and the same man, and yet somehow they weren't.

Luc had been exciting. Wild. Irresponsible. A man

Annie had known instinctively wouldn't make a good husband for her or any other woman, let alone a father to the baby she had discovered she was expecting.

Luca de Salvatore was something else, however....

Ruthless, powerful, completely confident of himself and his abilities, Luca de Salvatore would take his responsibilities as a father, at least, very seriously indeed.

He did take them seriously!

To the extent he was insisting that Annie marry him or risk a legal battle for Oliver.

How could she possibly have allowed herself to fall in love with him all over again?

'Annie...?' Luc frowned across at her as he saw that her thoughts—whatever they were—had made her face go pale, and her eyes take on a slightly haunted look. 'The doctor seems confident that Oliver will be able to go home in the morning.'

Those deep blue eyes now sparked at him angrily. 'Just in time for you to try and take him away from me!' She took a protective step towards the bed where Oliver slept.

Ahh...

Luc was sure that Annie had no idea how young and vulnerable she looked as she faced him so challengingly. Like a tigress protecting her young.

When they had met again at Lake Garda, and Luc learnt that she was Anna Balfour—one of the notoriously wayward daughters of Oscar Balfour—he had made assumptions about her character. About her fitness to be a mother to his son too, once he learnt of Oliver's existence.

Seeing her distress this afternoon over Oliver's

accident, her tension on the journey back to England, and then observing how tender and loving she was with the little boy once they had arrived at the hospital, Luc now realised how wrong he had been. Annie's love for Oliver was absolute. A fierce and protective love that would see Luc in hell before she would ever relinquish her son to him.

Just as it had only taken Luc one glance at Oliver, one touch of his delicate little hand, to be overwhelmed by that same fierce and protective love.

'Mummy?'

Luc's attention sharpened on the little boy in the bed as Oliver awoke for the first time, his eyes the same deep, deep blue as his mother's as he looked up at her so trustingly.

'Hello, darling,' she greeted him huskily, smiling as she sat on the side of the bed to gently brush a curl back from the little boy's brow. 'How are you feeling now?'

He pulled a face. 'My head hurts.'

Annie gazed down at him tenderly. 'Would you like me to go and ask the nurse to give you something to make the hurt go away?'

'Yes, please, Mummy.' Oliver gave a tentative smile.

Oliver looked *so* much like him at that age, Luc recognised achingly as he stood back from the bed watching Annie and Oliver together. The same dark curls. The same wide brow. The same shaped face.

Only the blue of his eyes was different.

Beautiful deep blue eyes.

Annie's eyes...

She looked across at him now, those eyes guarded. 'Would you sit with Oliver while I go and find a nurse?'

Luc could feel a nerve pulsing in his tightly clenched jaw as he nodded. 'Of course.'

She turned back to Oliver, giving his hand a little squeeze as she stood to move slightly away so that Luc was now visible to the little boy. 'Oliver, this is Luc. He—he's a friend of mine,' she added awkwardly.

Oliver turned curious blue eyes in Luc's direction. 'Hello,' he greeted solemnly.

There was a lump in Luc's throat that prevented him from answering immediately. An emotional surge that made breathing difficult.

'Luc?' Annie prompted, frowning at his continued silence.

What was wrong with him? Why didn't Luc say something? Was he annoyed because she had introduced him to Oliver as only a friend?

Well, that was just too bad because Annie had no intention of just blurting out, in what to Oliver was the middle of the night, that Luc was his father. There would be plenty of time for them to explain things to him once he was allowed home and was back amongst things, and people, that were familiar to him.

Which Luc certainly wasn't!

He seemed to give himself a mental shake before he stepped closer to Oliver's bed. 'I am very pleased to meet you, Oliver.' His voice was low and warm as he proffered his hand to the little boy.

A formality that Oliver obviously took delight in as he returned the gesture. 'Have you been to Italy with my mummy?' he asked curiously.

Annie raised mocking brows at Luc as she waited to see how he was going to deal with *that* question!

'I live in Italy, Oliver,' he answered.

Oliver's eyes widened. 'You do?'

Luc nodded. 'I am Italian. My full name is Luca de Salvatore.'

And you are my son…

Annie could almost hear those five unspoken words on the end of that sentence. Unspoken for now, that is.

She straightened abruptly. 'I'll be back in two minutes,' she promised firmly before hurrying from the room.

Luc scowled a little at the warning he had heard in her tone. As if she half expected him to claim Oliver as his son right here and now.

He forced a relaxed smile to his lips as he moved to take her place, sitting on the side of the bed. 'I believe that you had an argument with a horse earlier today?' he teased lightly.

'I lost!' Oliver grinned, revealing tiny, even white teeth.

Luc chuckled. 'So you did. But the doctor says you will have a most distinguishing scar once you have healed.'

The little boy thought about that for a moment before pulling a face. 'I didn't mean to worry Mummy.'

Luc gave him a reassuring smile. 'In my experience, mummies always worry.'

Oliver shook his head. 'My mummy smiles and laughs a lot.'

'Does she?'

The little boy nodded. 'Not when she has to go away on business for Granddad, of course. Then she frowns a lot, because she doesn't really want to go.'

Out of the mouths of babes and innocents…

The picture Oliver was painting of Anna Balfour as

his mother was one of warmth and love and laughter. With a definite aversion to going 'away on business for Granddad.'

Luc gave Oliver another reassuring smile. 'It wasn't for very long though, was it?'

Oliver shrugged. 'She still doesn't like it.'

Annie had told Luc that herself. Explained that she worked for her father because she was a single mother who, far from being one of the spoilt and wayward Balfour sisters, felt she had to work at something in order to pay her way in life. Even if it was doing something she didn't like.

Begging the question, what would Annie have done with her life if she hadn't become pregnant four and a half years ago?

If Luc hadn't left her alone and pregnant?

Luc's tension was so palpable when Annie came back into the room that she almost felt as if she could reach out and touch it, making her wonder what he and Oliver had been talking about in her absence.

'I brought you a coffee,' she told Luc as she crossed the room carrying the two cups. She almost spilled most of Luc's in the saucer when she felt the light touch of his fingers sliding against hers as he stood to take the hot drink from her. 'So how have you two been getting along in my absence?' Annie prompted brightly as she moved to stand beside her son.

Oliver beamed up at her. 'Luc says I'm going to have a dist…a distinshed scar when my cut gets better.'

'Distinguished,' Annie corrected automatically, deliberately keeping her gaze averted from Luc after her earlier reaction to just the touch of his fingers against hers. Although she couldn't help but be completely aware of him as he stood on the other side of the bed.

It wasn't fair, simply wasn't fair, that she responded in this way to Luc's slightest touch. Things would be so much easier for Annie if she could just have hated him.

Instead she had fallen in love with him. Again.

Which was going to make things very awkward when she refused to marry him and he attempted to try and take Oliver away from her.

They stood to one side as the nurse bustled into the room to check on Oliver before administering the liquid medicine that would help to ease his pain.

'Thank you for the coffee,' Luc murmured gruffly.

'You're welcome,' Annie dismissed as she continued to watch Oliver chat happily to the nurse.

Luc drew in a harsh breath at her coolness. 'Would you prefer it if I didn't stay here tonight?'

She snorted. 'What would your reaction be if I were to say yes?'

Luc smiled a little. 'Then I would respect your wishes and leave, of course.'

Her eyes were wide with disbelief as she finally looked up at him. 'Really?'

'I am not a monster, Annie,' he said quietly.

'I've never said that you are.'

'But you have thought it,' Luc guessed, grimly now.

Her mouth firmed as she looked away. 'Maybe.'

He drew in a sharp breath. 'Oliver is a beautiful child.'

'Yes, he is.'

'A beautiful and happy child.'

Her jaw tensed. 'Yes.'

'And you are obviously a wonderful mother.'

Annie turned to him impatiently, irritation creasing her brow. 'Knowing that isn't going to stop you from trying to take him away from me though, is it?' she hissed under her breath.

Luc frowned fiercely. 'You still reject the idea of marriage? Do you not feel that Oliver would benefit from living with both his parents?'

Her chin rose stubbornly. 'Not if it means I have to marry *you*, no! Now, if you'll excuse me…?' She put her empty cup down on the table. 'I would like to sit with Oliver until he falls asleep.' She moved back to Oliver's side now that the nurse had quietly left the room, sitting down to once again hold her son's hand as she murmured soft words of reassurance.

Luc remained standing across the room, for once in his ordered life completely at a loss as to how to proceed.

Marriage, and providing the necessary heirs to one day take over the reins of the de Salvatore business empire, had both been things Luc had envisaged for some time in the future. The far and distant future. Learning he already had a son had made him rethink those plans, dictating that he marry Anna Balfour now and legitimise his son. He had seen her refusal to marry him as merely an obstacle to be overcome. One that, if she persisted in her refusal, Luc would circumvent by instead legally claiming Oliver as his son and heir. The Balfour family might be rich and powerful, but the past four years had ensured that Luc was even more so!

It had been a decision, as with all the decisions Luc had made, based on cold, hard facts rather than emotions.

Luc certainly hadn't been prepared for how he would feel when he saw Oliver for the first time. The instantaneous and almost overwhelming feelings of love that had besieged and captured him in a single heartbeat.

The same overwhelming love that Annie so obviously felt for her son.

The same adoration that Oliver felt for the mother who had unselfishly loved and cared for him since the day he was born.

Was Luc now to be instrumental in these two warm and loving beings having to be torn apart from each other? Could he really do that to either of them?

To Oliver...

To Annie...

That same warm and passionate woman Luc had held in his arms only hours ago as the two of them made passionate love to each other.

Emotion had played no part in Luc's life over the past few years, and now he was beset with too many of them. Emotions that made a nonsense of cold logic and practicality. Emotions that made his heart ache and resulted in the breaking down of the barriers he had so painstakingly erected about his heart in his determination to rebuild the de Salvatore business empire until it was bigger and more powerful than it had ever been before...

'Luc? Luc!' Annie repeated more insistently as he seemed so lost in thought he didn't hear her the first time. 'Oliver is asleep now so we may as well try to grab a couple of hours' rest ourselves,' she explained softly as those narrowed dark eyes finally focused on her and asked a silent question.

No doubt Luc had been hatching plans as to the best

way to take Oliver away from her with the least trouble to himself, Annie surmised angrily.

He nodded his understanding. 'I will be back shortly.' He strode over to the door.

Annie frowned. 'Where are you going?'

'I need some fresh air before sleeping,' he paused to say before leaving.

Annie glared at the closed door for several long seconds, but there was very little point now that he'd gone. 'Fine,' she muttered to herself before grabbing her own overnight bag and going into the adjoining bathroom, closing the door firmly, but quietly, behind her.

There was no way, Annie told herself forcefully as she stared at her dishevelled reflection in the mirror over the sink, no way on this earth that she would ever allow Luc to take Oliver away from her and the family that loved him.

'I bet he's with his lawyer right now plotting and planning how best to take Oliver away from me!' Annie said furiously the next morning as she paced restlessly up and down Tilly's sitting room at the gatehouse in the grounds of Balfour Manor.

As promised, Oliver had been discharged from hospital earlier this morning, and a couple of hours ago Luc had driven the three of them to the gatehouse. Luc had then carried a sleepy Oliver up to his bedroom and seen him settled down for a nap before making his apologies and leaving to keep a business appointment in London.

Considering that Luc hadn't even known he was going to be in England today, to Annie's mind that business appointment could only be to discuss one thing!

'Perhaps you've misunderstood him, darling?' Tilly's worried frown totally belied her reasoning tone.

Annie gave her mother a pitying look. 'You can't really be this naive, Mummy. You were married to the original arrogant despot for four years, for goodness' sake!'

'I really can't allow you to talk about your father in that way, Annie. Besides, Oscar never once suggested taking my children away from me when we divorced,' Tilly defended her ex-husband.

'Only because he wouldn't have known what to do with us if he had!' she pointed out with some disgust.

Her mother tutted reprovingly. 'Annie, your father is my best friend.'

'I know that, Mummy.' She sighed heavily as she dropped down into an armchair. 'I'm sorry, I don't mean to upset you, I just—' She gave a frustrated growl. 'I didn't misunderstand Luc, Mummy. He was perfectly clear when he told me that I either become his wife or he will take his son away from me by other means.'

Luc had been completely uncommunicative when he'd returned from his walk outside the night before, and again this morning during the drive back to Balfour Manor.

Annie hadn't been feeling exactly chatty herself after spending an almost sleepless night alternately checking on Oliver and trying to ignore Luc's disturbing presence on top of the bed beside her own.

But she didn't need to be more than half awake to know the reason Luc had disappeared so abruptly to visit London so soon after arriving at Balfour Manor.

'Your father would *never* allow it—'

'I don't see how he can stop it when Luc is so obviously Oliver's father.' Annie scowled darkly, her fierce determination of the previous night severely depleted after her virtually sleepless night.

She wished she had her mother's optimism, she really did. But the more Annie thought about Luc's claim on Oliver, of the love she had seen burning brightly in the darkness of Luc's eyes as he looked at his son for the first time, the less sure Annie felt in her ability to stop him from taking Oliver from her.

Which left a loveless marriage between herself and Luc as the only other viable option—and one that Annie had been fighting against with every fibre of her being!

How could she possibly marry Luc when to him she was just part and parcel of a smooth and trouble-free claim on Oliver? When she was so hopelessly in love with him and he so clearly did not feel the same way about her?

'Yes, I've been longing to talk to you about that.' Her mother eyed her curiously. 'How on earth did you ever meet Luca de Salvatore in the first place, let alone— Well...' Tilly gave a rueful grimace.

'Go to bed with him?' Annie finished drily. 'Bad luck!' she muttered, almost to herself. 'Pure bad luck!'

'Not the most flattering description I have heard in regard to my bedroom skills,' Luc said as he strolled confidently into the drawing room, very dark and handsome in a white polo shirt and tailored black trousers. 'Mrs Williams,' he greeted a blushing Tilly with a mocking lift of his dark brows. 'Would you mind very much leaving Annie and me alone for a few minutes so that we might talk?'

'I have nothing to say to you,' Annie said defensively as she stood.

Luc regarded her through narrowed lids, noting the dark shadows beneath her eyes, and the pallor of her cheeks, no doubt both a result of Annie's lack of sleep the night before.

Luc hadn't slept at all the previous night either, his thoughts still deeply troubled despite the long walk he had taken outside in the fresh air. Annie's anguish as she lay beside him, dry-eyed but obviously deeply upset, had only added to that inner turmoil.

Only Luc's total physical awareness of Annie, and the knowledge that she would no doubt refuse any comfort he might offer, had prevented him from getting up from his own bed to lie beside her and take her in his arms.

That, and the doubt that he could control his awareness of her enough to offer her only comfort!

Even now, wearing a black T-shirt and fitted black jeans that did little to flatter her pallor or heavily tired eyes, Annie was still the most desirable woman Luc had ever known.

His mouth tightened. 'But *I* have a few things I wish to say to *you*,' he told her firmly.

She shrugged. 'I have already told my mother that it's your intention to apply for legal custody of Oliver.'

'I have no intention of applying for custody of Oliver,' Luc bit out.

Annie eyed him scathingly. 'You still think you can force me into marrying you?'

'No, I no longer think that either,' he acknowledged tautly.

Her eyes widened. 'Then—'

'Would you mind leaving us, Mrs Williams?' Luc asked again softly.

'Not at all.' Tilly rose gracefully to her feet. 'I'll only be in the laundry room, darling,' she reassured Annie warmly as she left, closing the door quietly behind her.

Leaving Luc as the sole focus of her daughter's frowning blue eyes.

CHAPTER TWELVE

'BUT I don't understand,' Annie said, looking puzzled.

Luc had said that he no longer intended applying for custody of Oliver and that he wasn't going to force Annie into marrying him either. So what was he going to do? Surely he didn't just expect the two of them to come and live with him in Rome?

He gave a rueful shrug. 'Tell me, Annie, how would you have felt, reacted, when we met again at Lake Garda, if there had been no Oliver to…complicate things, shall we say?'

Her cheeks flushed warmly. 'Even without Oliver, you would still have considered me one of the notorious Balfour sisters,' she reminded him.

Luc's jaw tightened. 'I asked how *you*, not I, would have felt about us meeting again if Oliver had not been a consideration.'

Exactly as she had felt even knowing of Oliver's existence; she had fallen in love with Luc all over again! No. Annie had realised that she had never actually ever stopped loving him.…

She spread out her hands in denial. 'I'm sorry, I can't envisage a world where Oliver doesn't exist.'

Luc drew in a harsh breath as Annie's words hit him

with the force of a blow to the chest. It had only been a matter of hours since Luc first looked at his son, but he could no longer imagine a world where Oliver did not exist either. Just as he could not imagine a world without Annie Balfour in it.

'He truly is an adorable child.'

'Yes, he is,' Annie confirmed huskily.

'All your own doing.'

'Oh, I think you'll find there were more people than me involved in that. Tilly. Oscar. My sisters,' she elaborated with a challenging look as Luc looked at her enquiringly.

Luc knew that Annie was right to feel the way that she did; he had judged all of those people, all of Annie's family, on the headlines that so often appeared about them in the newspapers.

But he had been wrong about Annie, and having now met Tilly Williams, he knew he had also been wrong concerning his assumptions about her; the chances were that he had also misjudged Oscar Balfour and his many daughters too.

He smiled. 'I am proud to call Oliver my son.'

'And so you should be!' Annie reproved indignantly.

That tigress protecting her cub again...

'You still have not answered my original question,' Luc reminded her.

'How would I have felt about meeting you again at Lake Garda if I hadn't become pregnant four and a half years ago?' Annie repeated drily. 'Hmm, let's see.' Her expression was rather mocking as she seemed to give the question some thought. 'I meet a wild and sexy Italian on the ski slopes—'

'Wild and sexy?' Luc choked, with a pained wince.

'Wild and sexy,' Annie repeated firmly, knowing that was exactly how Luc had appeared to her all those years ago. 'We ski down the mountain together. He invites me back to his chalet for some food and schnapps. We end up spending the night together. We part the following day having agreed to meet up again for dinner that evening. And then—poof!—this wild and sexy Italian does a disappearing act on me.' Her voice hardened angrily as she recalled her humiliation when Luc hadn't met her that evening as planned. When she had sat alone in the restaurant for more than an hour, sure that Luc would join her at any moment, and that he had just been unavoidably detained.

He had been *unavoidably detained* for four and a half years!

Luc frowned darkly. 'There was a very good reason why I did not meet you for dinner that evening—'

'Oh, I'm sure that there was,' Annie scorned, two bright spots of angry colour in her previously pale cheeks. 'Maybe you needed to wash your hair? Or there was something on the television you wanted to watch? Or maybe you just decided to move on to someone who was more of a challenge!' she accused, more than a little disgusted with herself.

Annie still burned with embarrassment every time she so much as thought about how easy a conquest she had been for Luc. A few sexy smiles, a caress, a kiss or two, and she had been putty in his hands!

She shook her head to clear the unpleasant thoughts from it. 'How would I have felt about seeing that man again a few years later? Exactly the same way I felt when

I saw you again two days ago, Luc—I wanted to punch you on your arrogant nose!'

Luc drew in a swift breath, knowing he deserved Annie's condemnation, that his behaviour had been utterly disgraceful. Even more so than he could ever have imagined when a child had resulted from their night together. A child that Annie had taken complete responsibility for. That she'd had no choice but to take responsibility for when Luc had disappeared so completely!

His jaw tightened. 'I owe you an explanation for the way I left so abruptly that day without leaving a message at the restaurant.'

'It's *way* too late for explanations!' she scoffed. 'So what if you had turned up for dinner that evening, Luc?' she continued impatiently as he would have protested. 'At most we might have had a few days' holiday fling before I had to return to England. Or we might have just met up again that evening and decided we didn't like each other enough to even bother with that.' She shrugged. 'Your method of ending things may have been a little callous, but on reflection your instinct not to continue the relationship was probably the correct one.'

Luc had asked for Annie's honesty, and he had absolutely no doubt he was getting it! 'If I had not left so suddenly you may at least have had the name of your baby's father!' he ground out.

'A name, maybe,' she accepted coolly. 'But knowing your name was Luca de Salvatore wouldn't have made any difference to the decisions I made once I discovered I was pregnant.'

Luc's eyes narrowed. 'You still would not have told me?'

Annie knew how angry Luc was by the way his

English had become more clipped and accented. 'I still wouldn't have told you,' she said truthfully.

'Why not?'

'Oh, for goodness' sake, Luc!' She made an impatient movement. 'This! This is why I wouldn't have told you! Because if I had, we would just have ended up having this same argument four years ago instead of now. You demanding that I marry you or you'll attempt to take Oliver away from me. I say *attempt*, because I have absolutely no intention of allowing you to win that particular battle,' she told him defiantly. 'Just as I won't marry a man just because he's the father of my child.'

It was the answer that Luc had expected. The only answer he could expect, when to Annie he would never be more than just the father of her child.

He lowered his lids to guard his expression. 'When we first met you were in the final year of an English degree—'

'I don't remember telling you that,' Annie cut in suspiciously.

'No.' Luc's mouth twisted. 'I knew no more about you then either than your first name and that you had a sexy unicorn tattoo on your lower back.'

'Then how? You've had me investigated!' Annie ignored the unicorn remark as her indignation rose. 'You hired some sleazy private investigator to tell you every little detail of my life!' The angry colour returned to her cheeks.

Luc winced. 'My assistant provided the necessary information, not a sleazy investigator.'

'It's the *why* rather than the *who* that interests me!' she challenged. 'Were you looking for something to use against me in a custody battle, Luc? Because if you were, then I can assure you that you were wasting your time! I—'

'I have told you there will be *no* custody battle, Annie,' Luc interrupted quickly.

'Because you still think you can bully me into marrying you!' she exclaimed.

Luc gave a rueful shake of his head. 'No, you have finally convinced me of your determination concerning that subject also.'

Annie paced the room restlessly. 'Then why did you have me investigated, Luc? Why were you asking me about my degree? What possible relevance can any of that have on the here and now?'

He shrugged muscled shoulders. 'I was curious as to what you would have done with that degree if you had not had Oliver.'

'Why were you?' She eyed him suspiciously.

Luc sighed his impatience. 'We would progress further with this conversation if you stopped being so defensive.'

'Defensive is how you make me feel, Luc,' she admitted heavily.

Luc was well aware of that. Just as he was aware that Annie had good reason to feel the way she did after his behaviour over these past two days.

'Could we perhaps just sit down for a few moments, take a couple of deep breaths and then talk calmly together like the two adults that we are?' he asked reasonably.

Could they? Somehow Annie doubted that very much. There was too much history between them, both past and present, for either of them to remain calm for very long.

'We can try,' she allowed grudgingly as she subsided into one of the armchairs.

'That is all that I ask,' Luc said ruefully as he did the same. 'What was your purpose in taking an English degree? I cannot believe it was with the intention of working for your father.'

'Hardly,' Annie drawled drily. 'No—' she rested her head back against the chair '—I wanted to teach, and maybe become the twenty-first-century Jane Austen in my spare time.'

Luc raised surprised brows. 'Teach and write?'

Annie glanced across at him. 'Yes,' she confirmed shortly. 'But instead my father has decided it's now time to groom me into becoming part of the upper management of his business empire.' She gave a horrified grimace.

'You have a natural talent for it, I believe.' Luc nodded. 'I have already implemented the deficiencies you noted at my hotel in Lake Garda,' he explained at Annie's questioning look.

Her eyes widened. 'You have?'

He gave a rueful smile. 'I talked with the manager yesterday.'

'Oh.'

'But having a natural talent for something does not mean it is what you should do,' Luc continued. 'Oliver told me that you do not like going away on business for your father.'

'Did he?' Annie gave an affectionate smile at the thought of her young son. 'He's right, of course. Oh, I have no doubts that I'm more than capable of doing the job—'

'But?'

'But—' she gave a weary sigh '—it really wasn't what I envisaged for my future when I was eighteen.'

'I am sure that at eighteen you did not envisage becoming a single mother by the age of twenty-one either!' Luc pointed out.

Annie calmly met the dark glitter of his gaze. 'I have never regretted having Oliver, Luc. Not even for a moment,' she added for emphasis.

No, Luc didn't believe that she had. 'What if you could have both?' he asked softly. 'If you could be a mother to Oliver but still fulfil your own dreams of teaching and writing at the same time?'

'Which I could do by marrying you, no doubt,' Annie said knowingly.

'No doubt.' Luc gave a humourless smile. 'But we have already ruled that out, have we not?'

'I have, yes, but I'm still not sure you have.'

Luc could hear the wariness in her tone. A wariness he well deserved. 'Annie, I went to London to see my English lawyer this morning, in order to have him draw up the necessary custody documents—'

'I *knew* it!' She stood suddenly, her gaze accusing as she glared down at him. 'This was what you've been planning, isn't it? Have me investigated, find something you can use against me—although I have no idea what that could be when I've lived like a nun for the past four years—and then force me into signing the papers that give you custody of Oliver! Well, I'm not signing anything, Luc. Not now! Not *ever*!' She clenched her hands to hide the way they were shaking.

Luc had no doubt as to the depth of Annie's anger. He could see it in the furious glitter of her blue eyes, the flush to her cheeks and the stubborn set to her chin.

Just as he was aware of a slight lifting of the heaviness inside him at the knowledge that Annie had 'lived like a nun' these past years. Although her behaviour yesterday afternoon when they'd returned from their motorbike ride could not exactly have been deemed nunlike.

'As usual you have chosen to misunderstand me.' He sighed.

'Somehow I doubt that!' she argued.

Luc gave a weary shake of his head. 'The documents I am having drawn up do not involve my taking Oliver from you but instead give you full custody of him, with reasonable visiting rights for me, when and if you, as his mother, allow it.'

Annie stared at him. Completely stunned. Her mind had gone utterly blank.

'They will also make financial provision for both you and Oliver, so that you do not feel you have to work at anything if you do not wish to do so,' Luc added evenly.

What?

'I don't understand,' Annie finally managed to stutter, looking dazed.

Luc raised an eyebrow. 'I am going to financially provide for both you and Oliver rather than fight you for custody of him.'

'Why?' she asked, still eyeing him warily.

'Because it is the right thing to do,' Luc said through gritted teeth. 'Because I no longer believe I have the right to take Oliver from you.' He flexed tense shoulders. 'Until I saw Oliver yesterday he was not quite real to me as a person in his own right. A little boy with feelings and needs of his own. Watching the two of you together, that special bond that you both have, understanding the sacrifices that you have made in your own life since he was born, I realised that I have no right to even attempt to take him away from you.' His expression was bleak. 'That I gave up that right four and a half years ago when I disappeared so abruptly out of your life and left you alone to cope with the results of our night together.'

Emotions warred deep within Annie. Feelings of elation that Luc no longer wanted to even try to take Oliver from her, let alone force her into marrying him. Followed by the intense pain of knowing that Luc's capitulation meant he was going to walk out of her life for a second time, the only contact they had in future years when he came to collect Oliver or return him to her.

Years when Annie would have to stand back and watch Luc marry someone else. Have children with someone else. Grow old with someone else. Love someone else...

She swallowed hard. 'You said you had a good reason for disappearing that day four and a half years ago?' she recalled huskily.

'I considered it a good reason at the time,' he acknowledged. 'But not an acceptable one when compared to what you have suffered because your "wild and sexy" Italian lover was also a very selfish one!'

'Hey, I've never considered myself to have suffered because I chose to have Oliver,' Annie chided him. 'Nothing can compare to the privilege I feel at being his mother. He has been the biggest joy, the most wonderful experience, of my entire life.'

Once again Luc experienced that ache in his chest at the knowledge of Annie's unconditional love for Oliver. For his son, and not for him.

'Perhaps,' he began hoarsely, 'once we have dealt with

the legalities of Oliver's custody, you might consider having dinner with me one evening?'

Her eyes widened. 'You want us to have dinner together?' she echoed slightly incredulously.

Luc held her gaze as he nodded. 'I would like that very much, yes.'

Annie felt somewhat punch-drunk as she was hit with one surprise after another. She had only just begun to believe that Luc was no longer going to fight her for custody of Oliver, or force her into a loveless marriage, and now he sounded as if he were asking her out on a date!

'Why didn't you meet me for dinner that night?' she probed slowly.

Luc drew in a harsh breath. 'What can I say? You were right to describe me as being wild then. Not only wild but deeply irresponsible too,' he added honestly. 'As I have told you, it was an irresponsibility that ultimately resulted in my almost ruining my father's business empire. It did result in my father's near-fatal heart attack,' he added bleakly.

Annie's eyes widened. 'It happened *then*? That's the reason you disappeared so suddenly instead of meeting me for dinner?'

'Yes.' A nerve pulsed in Luc's tightly clenched jaw. 'I had left Rome only days earlier, like the defiant and spoilt young man that I was, leaving my father to deal with the mess I left behind me. It almost killed him,' he said flatly.

Annie knew a little of the guilt and pain Luc must be feeling—the same pain and guilt she had felt when she had to tell her own father that she was pregnant. The same determination she had felt to atone for her mistake by agreeing to work for Oscar, even though it wasn't what she really wanted to do.

The same pain and guilt that had resulted in a single-minded, ruthless determination developing in Luc, consequently making him into the hard, implacable man he was today.

The man Annie knew herself to have fallen in love with all over again...

But at least she now knew the reason Luc had left her sitting alone in that restaurant. 'So would you turn up this time?' she asked lightly.

Luc frowned. 'Sorry?'

'If I agree to have dinner with you, are you going to turn up this time?' she murmured ruefully.

She still had no idea why Luc had issued the invitation, but loving him as she did, and having his assurances that the heavy weight of Oliver's custody had been removed from the equation, it certainly wasn't an invitation Annie intended turning down.

Luc gave the ghost of a smile. 'You will never know how much I regret not meeting you at the restaurant that night.'

Annie looked at him searchingly. Wishing she could read what was behind those enigmatic dark eyes. Wishing she knew why Luc had issued this invitation.

Well, there was only one way she could find out the answer to that! 'If you're only asking me out to dinner so that we can discuss Oliver—'

'I would be more than happy to talk about Oliver—the sheer miracle of him!—twenty-four hours a day,' Luc admitted. 'But alternatively, I—we—do not have to talk about him at all. I want to spend time with you, Annie. To get to know *you* better. And for you to get to know me. You have turned my world upside down these past two days,' he added emotionally.

'Because of Oliver—'

'No, *not* because of Oliver!' Luc insisted.

How could he explain this to Annie? How could he make her understand the things he had discovered about himself yesterday evening when he'd gone outside and strolled so restlessly about the hospital grounds?

That it was she, and she alone, who had effected the changes in him. That since he had met her again she had completely demolished the barrier he had kept so tightly wrapped about his emotions. That his emotions were now so fully engaged, so exposed, he felt vulnerable in a way he had not believed possible.

Somehow Luc knew he had to try—more than try!— to make Annie believe these things, or risk losing her for ever.

'Annie, my dinner invitation has nothing to do with Oliver,' Luc said firmly. 'I am asking that you give me a chance to…to court you, if you will, in the old-fashioned way.'

She became very still. 'Why?' she breathed.

Luc drew in a ragged breath and decided to risk everything on one last throw of the dice. 'Because I love you. Because since meeting you again two days ago I have come to admire and love you more than any other woman on earth. Because the thought of having to allow you to walk out of my life for a second time is totally destroying me!' His hands were tightly clenched at his sides, his jaw clamped together so tightly that it looked in danger of snapping from the pressure.

Annie stared at him. Simply stared. Rendered completely and utterly dumbstruck by what Luc had just said. By how he looked.

The pained darkness of his eyes, and the tension in his face and body were all clear testament to how important Annie's response to his declaration was to him.

Luc *loved* her?

Somehow, during the confusion and pain of the past two days, Luc had managed to fall in love with her?

But why not? After all, hadn't she fallen in love with him all over again during those same two days?

Still she hesitated. 'Are you sure this doesn't have anything to do with Oliver?'

Luc released his breath in a rush. 'Doesn't the fact that I am signing over full custody of Oliver to you, relinquishing all right to him other than the ones you allow me, tell you that it does not? That I am doing those things because I cannot bear the thought of hurting you? Any more than I have already, of course,' he added wryly. 'Annie—' he stepped forward to place his hands lightly on her shoulders as he looked down at her intently '—all I am asking is the chance, the opportunity, to—'

'Court me,' Annie finished evenly, a bubble of happiness, pure unadulterated happiness, beginning to rise within her.

'It's hopeless, isn't it?' he groaned softly, releasing her to run an agitated hand through the dark thickness of his hair. 'Why am I even bothering to say these things to you? Of course you do not wish to go out to dinner with me. Do not want us to get to know each other better.' His expression was grim. 'Why should you want me anywhere near you when I have either threatened or made love to you since the moment we first met again?' He shook his head. 'I am sorry, Annie. So very, very sorry!'

He turned sharply on his heel, his expression bleak as he left the room.

Annie couldn't move for several seconds, the closing of the front door what finally galvanised her into action as she hurried into the hallway and wrenched that door open.

Luc's back was towards her as he stood in the driveway unlocking his car. 'Where are you going?' she demanded dazedly.

His shoulders stiffened before he turned slowly to face her. 'I will be back.' He grimaced. 'I just need some time to myself. As you, no doubt, need some time away from me.' His eyes were no longer black and remorseless but the colour of warm chocolate, and that telltale nerve pulsed in his tightly clenched cheek.

The bubble of happiness inside Annie became bigger, and then bigger still, until she felt full to bursting with it.

She leant against the door frame. 'You know, Luc, you've done nothing the past couple of minutes but ask questions and then answer them yourself. If you carry on like this I may have to attempt another judo throw on you just so that I can get a word in edgewise,' she teased, remembering exactly what had happened the last time she had tried that.

It was obvious Luc also remembered as his expression softened slightly as he answered her. 'This time I would probably let you succeed.'

'*Let* me succeed?' Annie echoed drily. 'Now there's a challenge if ever I heard one!' She walked slowly down the path towards him.

Luc looked down at her as she came to a halt in front of him, the sunlight picking out the gleaming red highlights in her hair, and her eyes the clear blue of the Caribbean Sea in a youthfully beautiful face.

Annie was so petite, and yet at the same time so very strong; she had to be to have stood up to him the past two days! So young and yet at the same time so wise and knowing.

And she held Luc's heart in the palms of her tiny hands...

He reached out to grasp both of those hands in his. 'I really am sorry for the way I have behaved towards you, Annie.'

'How sorry?'

'*Very* sorry.'

'And...?'

'I really am very, very sorry?'

'And...?' she repeated with some frustration.

Luc gave a pained frown. 'I do not understand.'

Annie sighed. 'That was your cue to repeat your dinner invitation. In fact, it was an invitation for you to repeat all your questions. Oh, what the hell!' she dismissed, throwing her arms joyously about Luc's neck as she finally allowed her happiness to show. 'Forget the questions—my answer is yes!' She beamed up at him glowingly.

Luc's arms moved possessively about the slenderness of her waist as he looked down at her hungrily. 'You will allow me to take you out? To court you? To show you how much I have come to love you?'

'Yes. No. And very much yes,' Annie answered, more light-hearted than she had felt for a very long time. 'Any time, any place!'

Luc loved her.

He really loved her.

Annie knew—had absolutely no doubts—that nothing else on earth could have convinced Luc to back down from continuing to pursue his claim on Oliver unless he loved her very, very much.

'Yes, I may take you out to dinner?' Luc said slowly. 'No, I may not court you? And yes, I may show you how very much I have come to love you?'

'You forgot "any time, any place."' Annie grinned up at him unabashedly. 'Of course now, and Tilly's front garden, may not be the time or the place,' she added teasingly. 'But just as soon as we can be alone somewhere together—definitely yes!'

Luc became very still as he stared down uncertainly into the beautiful glow of Annie's face. 'I want you to marry me, Annie, not just make love with me.'

'That's why I don't think the old-fashioned courting is a good idea,' she chided happily, sobering when she could see that Luc still truly didn't understand. 'You don't need to court me, Luc.' She reached up and tenderly touched the side of his face. 'I already love you and want to marry you,' she revealed huskily.

Luc looked stunned for a second, then the hunger in his eyes deepened as Annie allowed him to see all the love for him she had been keeping in check. For so long, it seemed.

But no more. Now she could kiss Luc. Hold him. Tell him exactly how much and for how long she had loved him.

Something she proceeded to do to both their satisfaction…

Two weeks later

'Cheer up, Daddy.' Annie turned to smile at her father as the two of them sat on the terrace at the de Salvatore vineyard near Venice watching Luc in the pool as he attempted to teach Oliver how to swim. Oscar had given the three of them some time alone together before joining them in Italy to celebrate the announcement of Annie and Luc's engagement. 'Look on it as gaining a son rather than losing a daughter!'

'I'm not in the least unhappy at the thought of having Luca de Salvatore as my son-in-law,' Oscar assured with a smile, still a handsome man despite being in his early sixties. 'Especially as it's what I hoped would happen when I sent you to that particular business conference at Lake Garda,' he added softly.

Annie turned to him. *'What?'*

Oscar took one of her hands in his. 'You didn't really think that I would just accept it when you refused to tell me the name of your baby's father, did you?'

Well, of course Annie had thought he had!

Actually, had she? Had she really believed that her arrogant and powerful father wouldn't try to find out for himself exactly who Oliver's father might be?

'You've known *all this time* that Luc was Oliver's father?' she said disbelievingly.

Oscar shrugged. 'My enquiries at the time only showed that he was at the ski resort the same time as you were. But that equally applied to a lot of other men. But then I actually saw Luc across a restaurant in New York and... He and Oliver do bear a startling likeness to each other, don't you think?' He gazed affectionately at his grandson as Oliver giggled happily at something Luc had said to him.

Annie should have known; she should have guessed that her father had had an ulterior motive for sending her to the business conference in Italy!

'You aren't going to be annoyed with me over this, are you, Annie?' her father asked as he saw the way her eyes were sparkling. 'After all, I only made it possible for you and Luc to meet again. What happened then was up to the two of you.'

How could Annie possibly be angry with Oscar when 'what happened then' was the best thing that had ever happened in her life?

The past two weeks of being together had more than convinced Annie that it was her that Luc loved. Totally. To distraction.

Just as Annie loved him in the same way.

As they both adored their son.

And she had no doubts they would continue to love each other, and Oliver, and any more children that might result from their wholehearted commitment to each other.

'Mummy, come and join us!'

She looked up at Oliver as he held on to the poolside looking at her, the cut on his head having totally healed, thank goodness, the pleasure written all over his face at being with his beloved Daddy, as he was already calling Luc.

'Yes, Annie, come and join us,' Luc entreated as he joined Oliver at the side of the pool, looking much younger and more relaxed, his dark eyes warmly caressing as he made no effort to hide his complete adoration of her.

'Go!' Oscar encouraged indulgently as Annie stood to look down at him questioningly.

Annie didn't need to be told twice, running to the side of the pool to dive smoothly into the water, surfacing to laugh happily as Luc immediately caught her up in his arms and began kissing her.

Annie had finally faced her fears, and what she had discovered was Luc. The man she would love for the rest of her life and who would love her in the same way in return.

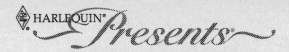

Coming Next Month

from **Harlequin Presents® EXTRA.** Available January 11, 2011.

#133 THE MAN BEHIND THE MASK
Maggie Cox
From Rags to Riches

#134 MASTER OF BELLA TERRA
Christina Hollis
From Rags to Riches

#135 CHAMPAGNE WITH A CELEBRITY
Kate Hardy
One Night at a Wedding

#136 FRONT PAGE AFFAIR
Mira Lyn Kelly
One Night at a Wedding

Coming Next Month

from **Harlequin Presents®.** Available January 25, 2011.

#2969 GISELLE'S CHOICE
Penny Jordan
The Parenti Dynasty

#2970 BELLA AND THE MERCILESS SHEIKH
Sarah Morgan
The Balfour Brides

#2971 HIS FORBIDDEN PASSION
Anne Mather

#2972 HIS MAJESTY'S CHILD
Sharon Kendrick

#2973 GRAY QUINN'S BABY
Susan Stephens
Men Without Mercy

#2974 HIRED BY HER HUSBAND
Anne McAllister

REQUEST YOUR
FREE BOOKS!

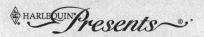 HARLEQUIN *Presents*

PASSION GUARANTEED SEDUCTION

2 FREE NOVELS PLUS
2 FREE GIFTS!

YES! Please send me 2 FREE Harlequin Presents® novels and my 2 FREE gifts (gifts are worth about $10). After receiving them, if I don't wish to receive any more books, I can return the shipping statement marked "cancel." If I don't cancel, I will receive 6 brand-new novels every month and be billed just $4.05 per book in the U.S. or $4.74 per book in Canada. That's a saving of at least 15% off the cover price! It's quite a bargain! Shipping and handling is just 50¢ per book.* I understand that accepting the 2 free books and gifts places me under no obligation to buy anything. I can always return a shipment and cancel at any time. Even if I never buy another book, the two free books and gifts are mine to keep forever.

106/306 HDN E5M4

Name _____ (PLEASE PRINT) _____

Address _____ Apt. # _____

City _____ State/Prov. _____ Zip/Postal Code _____

Signature (if under 18, a parent or guardian must sign)

Mail to the **Harlequin Reader Service:**
IN U.S.A.: P.O. Box 1867, Buffalo, NY 14240-1867
IN CANADA: P.O. Box 609, Fort Erie, Ontario L2A 5X3

Not valid for current subscribers to Harlequin Presents books.

Are you a current subscriber to Harlequin Presents books and want to receive the larger-print edition? Call 1-800-873-8635 today!

* Terms and prices subject to change without notice. Prices do not include applicable taxes. N.Y. residents add applicable sales tax. Canadian residents will be charged applicable provincial taxes and GST. Offer not valid in Quebec. This offer is limited to one order per household. All orders subject to approval. Credit or debit balances in a customer's account(s) may be offset by any other outstanding balance owed by or to the customer. Please allow 4 to 6 weeks for delivery. Offer available while quantities last.

Your Privacy: Harlequin Books is committed to protecting your privacy. Our Privacy Policy is available online at www.eHarlequin.com or upon request from the Reader Service. From time to time we make our lists of customers available to reputable third parties who may have a product or service of interest to you. If you would prefer we not share your name and address, please check here. ☐

Help us get it right—We strive for accurate, respectful and relevant communications. To clarify or modify your communication preferences, visit us at www.ReaderService.com/consumerschoice.

HP10R

*Harlequin Romance author Donna Alward is loved
for her gorgeous rancher heroes.*

*Meet Wyatt as he's confronted by both a precious
little pink bundle left on his doorstep and his neighbor Elli
who's going to show him the ropes....*

Introducing
PROUD RANCHER, PRECIOUS BUNDLE

THE SQUAWKING QUIETED as Elli picked the baby up, and
Wyatt turned around, trying hard to ignore the feelings of
inadequacy as Darcy immediately stopped fussing.

"Maybe she's uncomfortable. What do you think, sweet-
heart?" Elli turned her conversation to the baby.

"What do you think is wrong?" Wyatt asked, putting the
coffee pot back on the burner.

A strange look passed over Elli's face, one that looked
like guilt and panic. But it was gone quickly. "I couldn't
say," she replied.

"But you were so good with her this afternoon." Wyatt
put his hands on his hips.

"Lucky, that's all. I just…remembered a few things."
The same strange look flitted over her features once more.

Wyatt took the coffee to the table. "You fooled me. You
looked like you knew exactly what you were doing." So
much so that Wyatt had felt completely inept. A feeling he
despised. He was used to being the one in control.

Elli and Darcy walked the length of the kitchen and
back. After a few moments, she admitted, "I haven't really
cared for a baby before. The things I thought of were simply
things I'd heard about. Not from experience, Mr. Black."

Her chin jutted up, closing the subject but making him

want to ask the questions now pulsing through his mind. But then he remembered the old saying—*Don't look a gift horse in the mouth.* He'd benefit from whatever insight she had and be glad of it.

"I don't really know what babies need," he said. "I fed her, patted her back like you did, walked her to sleep, but every time I put her down…"

Wyatt almost groaned. Of course. He'd forgotten one important thing. He'd been so focused on getting the formula the right temperature that he'd forgotten to check her diaper. Not that he had any clue what to do there either.

Pulling calves and shoveling out stalls was far less intimidating than one tiny newborn.

"She's probably due for a diaper change, isn't she." He tried to sound nonchalant. This was a perfect opportunity. Elli must know how to change a diaper. He could simply watch her so he'd know better for the next time.

Instead, Elli came around the corner of the counter and placed Darcy back in his arms. "Here you go, Uncle Wyatt," she said lightly. "You get diaper duty. I'll fix the coffee. Cream and sugar?"

Oh boy, Wyatt thought, looking down into Darcy's pursed face, his smug plan blown to smithereens. He was in for it now.

Will sparks fly between Elli and Wyatt?

Find out in
PROUD RANCHER, PRECIOUS BUNDLE

Available February 2011 from Harlequin Romance

Try these Healthy and Delicious Spring Rolls!

INGREDIENTS

2 packages rice-paper
spring roll wrappers
(20 wrappers)

1 cup grated carrot

¼ cup bean sprouts

1 cucumber, julienned

1 red bell pepper, without
stem and seeds, julienned

4 green onions
finely chopped—
use only the green part

DIRECTIONS

1. Soak one rice-paper wrapper
   in a large bowl of hot water
   until softened.

2. Place a pinch each of carrots,
   sprouts, cucumber, bell
   pepper and green onion on the
   wrapper toward the bottom
   third of the rice paper.

3. Fold ends in and roll tightly
   to enclose filling.

4. Repeat with remaining
   wrappers. Chill before
   serving.

Find this and many more delectable recipes
including the perfect dipping sauce in

NTRSERIESJAN